…*I detach from my escort, slide into a seat across from him. He's not shackled or restrained in any way. He wears a grey sweatshirt and blue jeans. Clean-shaven, with short, cropped hair, balding on top. The chair scrapes when I move it in closer to the table. His eyes are blue and they stare at me from under thick, bushy brows.*

"*You look like yer old man," he says.*

*He doesn't offer his hand and I'm glad. Those hands have killed, obeying orders transmitted by a brain incapable of remorse. Those hands right there. Knobby with age, thin and pale and veined. Which finger pulled the trigger? What sort of mind could rationalize such a terrible command?*

# Disloyal Son:
## A False Memoir

CLIFF BURNS

Cover design: Chris Kent

Interior layout and design: Jana Rade, Impact Studios (Canada)

Published by Black Dog Press (blackdogpress@yahoo.ca)

Printed by: Lightning Source

ISBN: 978-0-9694853-9-1

Also by Cliff Burns:

*Sex & Other Acts of the Imagination* (stories)
*Exceptions & Deceptions* (stories)
*New & Selected Poems* (1985-2011)
*Stromata: Prose Works* (1992-2011)
*The Last Hunt*
*Of the Night*
*So Dark the Night*
*Righteous Blood*
*The Reality Machine* (stories)

BLACK DOG PRESS

*for Colleen*

"Never trust an Irishman, son:
he'll lie if it makes for a better story."

W.C.B.

# *"Please allow me to introduce myself..."*

Blame the whole thing on my father.

The Prince of Liars.

Throughout our childhood, he told my sister Connie and me God knows how many tall tales about his life and exploits. I'm not talking about a few assorted anecdotes, but a fully realized past, an alternate history filled with vivid images and recollections. I can remember watching some John Wayne war flick on TV and idly inquiring if he'd ever been a soldier.

"Sure, in Korea," came his immediate reply, "want to see my scars?" He rolled up a pant leg, showing me a divot on his shin then, beckoning me closer, parted his hairline, revealing a long, raised ridge near the crown. "Artillery attack," he explained. "The Chi-Coms pinpointed our position, nearly wiped us out." I must have looked properly impressed because he patted my head playfully. "But your old man managed to survive, never fear. Somehow I always walk away in the end." I demanded he show me the scars and repeat the story many times over the years and he always obliged, sometimes adding a few more details about his pal Smitty or Sergeant Spence, a man he claimed to simultaneously fear and love.

Except…when I wrote for my father's war records a few years after his death, I was informed by an official in Ottawa that no individual of that name and date of birth had ever served in any capacity in the Canadian military. In war or peace. The missive was brisk, polite, officious, a masterpiece of bureaucratic concision.

On other occasions dad told us that he'd: prospected for gold in Alaska, hunted whales off Nantucket and once played an afternoon of "cut throat" pool with the Right Honourable John G. Diefenbaker.

"A terrible loser," he confided, "swore like a drunken sailor."

And then one day, out of the blue, he told my sister and I never to let on but, in fact, we were descendants of nobility. "Our family used to own big estates in Scotland

and a manor house just outside Belfast. We had titles and everything, mind. My parents kept the papers in a leather case, I remember seeing it when I was a kid. Stamped with a royal seal, all legal and impressive. But it got lost in the big flood so now there's no proof..."

Our family line included knights and dukes, even an earl or two. Supposedly, we had our own coat of arms (he intended to do the research and track it down some day).

I mostly kept this latest revelation from my friends—I didn't want them treating me any different merely because I happened to have royal roots—but couldn't help mentioning it to my mother. After all, she was in on the secret too.

Phyllis paused, in the process of sliding a fried egg on to my plate. "He told you *what*?"

Later, when confronted, my father refused to recant. "*Of course* she'd say that, son. She doesn't want you putting on airs. We'll fly over there some time, the four of us, and I'll show you the place. It would still be ours if our stupid bloody ancestors hadn't backed the wrong horse or pissed it away on drink and dissipation." In the end, he convinced me. I'm afraid I began to speak in a bit of a posh voice. My friends tolerated me but I don't know why.

Connie was older and more skeptical. She was barely twelve when she offered this devastating critique of our father: "The problem with dad is that he doesn't want to be seen as just another ordinary, boring joe, with a safe, comfortable life and no identity." Nodding at her own sagacity.

Keep in mind that at the time all we knew about dad's vocation was that he held some vague position with the city of Kingston. Something to do with "public works" (whatever that was). His boss was Mr. Donahue. As to what exactly his duties entailed or what his official job description was, well, that information didn't overly concern us.

"You think he makes all that stuff up? About his past?"

Connie smiled knowingly. "I think he'd rather be mysterious, like Uncle Eugene. You notice how they stop talking about him when we're around? It's like we're supposed to forget he ever existed. He was dad's *brother*, for God's sake." Lowering her voice. "Even if he did kill himself, so what? Does that mean we should act like nothing happened? Erase our memories or whatever?"

"I remember that time he took us driving. He had a big Pontiac," I recalled, "but he refused to speed. Remember? We kept yelling 'faster, faster' but he wouldn't. Dad would've been tearing up the road." But Connie was right, talking about Eugene, swapping memories about our deceased uncle, wasn't permitted. And there were hints that aspects of Eugene's life bothered my father. Stuff we weren't supposed to know about. Once I came into the kitchen in the midst of one of their discussions and heard dad lamenting: "I wish he could have gotten away from them like I did. Got out from under their thumbs."

My mother demurred. "It was his life, Terry. We make our own beds and have to deal with the consequences."

"Yeah, but maybe he didn't have any choice because of the way he—" At that point one of them spotted me and they shut things down. Waiting until I'd left the room before continuing their dialogue.

Connie, naturally, was the first to put it all together. The half-heard conversations, code words, body language. Infrequent get-togethers with cousins and extended family also proved beneficial.

"Uncle Eugene was a big-time gangster," she informed me one afternoon, dropping her bombshell with the ease and aplomb of a seasoned news anchor.

I recall that day with almost crystalline clarity. We were at the Parkridge house, on the back deck. We'd moved from Ontario earlier in the year, enduring part of a prairie winter (finding it not at all to our liking). We were still getting used to the place but coping in our separate ways.

Dad had strung a hammock, which Connie promptly claimed as her personal domain under penalty of death (living up to her regal lineage). It was late June, a hot

Saskatchewan summer day. Not a whisper of wind. The cover was off the pool and the water was in, blue-tinted and shimmering invitingly, but something was wrong with the pump. Dad didn't want us swimming until the water had been properly filtered and chlorinated.

"You mean, like the Mafia?" By then I'd seen quite a few episodes of TV crime shows (dad was a big fan), so I wasn't *completely* out to lunch.

"What else?"

I was puzzled. "But…he wasn't Italian."

She popped a dozen sunflower seeds into her mouth. "Don't you know there're different gangs? Black and white, all races have 'em."

Which made sense to me. And I could see how the pieces fit. The secrecy and the way our folks discouraged any reference to a man who was once part of our circle, my father's *brother*. "D'you think he ever killed anybody?"

"Did he look like a killer to you?" Well, no. The last time I'd seen my uncle was at Aunt Gloria's, back in Kingston, a month or so before he died. He joined us for part of the day, the occasion a family gathering of some kind, likely celebrating an anniversary or the betrothal of a distant relative. When I say "family", I refer to a querulous congregation of extended kin who weren't very close despite their alleged blood ties. Such get-togethers usually ended in tears and recriminations, if not a fistfight.

And then we'd form up and do it all over again six months later.

Eugene wasn't himself that day. He barely spoke and seemed at least a third smaller than dad, reserved, withdrawn, already in the process of fading away. As he was leaving, he slipped Connie and me an American twenty-dollar bill each and told us not to spend it in one place. Which only confirmed our high opinion of the man.

But now Connie was telling me that money was tainted, practically dripping blood. The image thrilled and excited me. Eugene may not have walked around with a pistol under his coat, frequently slinking into the nearest dark alley to shake off pursuers, but he still became a figure of abiding interest to me. Employing the ruse that I was working on a school project, I cornered my father in the garage not long afterward and tried to pry some family history out of him.

"What did Uncle Eugene do?"

"*Do?*" Feigning puzzlement to buy time.

"Yeah, like, for a living."

"He, uh, y'know, he worked, he had a good job."

"Yes," I went along patiently, addressing him as I would a young child or a person considered somewhat dim, "but doing *what*?"

"Construction and, uh, infrastructure," he stated, with a marked lack of confidence.

"Like bridges, roads—"

"Right, right." Anxious to move on to the next line of query.

"In and around Kingston."

"Yeah. For the city. We both worked for the city, you know that."

"Did he build stuff or—"

"God, no." His patience showing signs of fraying, "Gene hated getting his hands dirty. Wouldn't know one end of a hammer from another."

"So what did he *do*?" I repeated.

"He…made sure things got done. Like a supervisor. For the city, mind."

"But what was his actual position?"

"How the hell should I know?" Throwing up his hands, frustrated at my stupid persistence.

That was as far as I got with him.


"—came over here from the old country back in the early Thirties. Settled around Lansdowne, bought a farm, raised dairy cows and did pretty well for themselves." She paused. "You're not writing any of this down."

"I'll remember," I said.

"Why don't you ask your dad about this?"

I made a face. "He'd start telling me that we own half of Ireland or we're related to Sean Connery or something." She had to smile. "Why did they leave Ireland in the first place? And why come to Canada?"

"They knew people here, relatives and such. The Webbs and Calhouns—you met some of them, you know who I mean. And it was getting bad over there, bad things were happening. They'd been given warnings, told they had to get out or else."

"Were they involved in politics or—"

"Honestly, I don't know, you'd have to ask his Lordship. It's a messed up country and there's all sorts of religious and political stuff too complicated to explain. Most of it goes right over my head. I don't think he much cares about it either."

"Dad says he hardly remembers anything about his life over there. Or maybe it's just that he doesn't like talking about it…"

"He told me about his father taking him down to the shipyard when he was a toddler. Carrying him on his shoulders so he could see better. That's where they built the *Titanic*, y'know."

"I guess he was still pretty young when they left."

"Just a wee runt. Him and Gene both. And Gloria nothing but a baby. Mostly Terry remembers being seasick. Puking the entire way over. He looked so bad his folks worried they wouldn't let him in the country. The customs agents would think he had some kind of disease."

"You said they knew people here?"

"Some. Mostly in the Ottawa area. Lots of Micks around there. Hamilton too. They took out a loan for the farm and paid it back in eight years. That's the family legend, anyway. And no collateral, apparently your grand-father's handshake was good enough for the bank." She pulled a face and I had to laugh.

"So…they had the farm and that was successful but none of the kids wanted to take over, so they sold every-thing and moved to Gananoque. Is that right?"

"Only for a year or so, then Terry's father got a job at the big train assembly plant and they moved to Kingston. Which is where we met and the story *really* begins…"

"Was it a blind date or—"

"Oh, no, I met him through Gene. I knew Gene before I knew Terry. I thought you knew that." I hadn't. *In-teresting*. "A bunch of us used to go dancing or see movies together. Just friends, having a good time. That's how I got involved with Gene, Terry, Gloria, that whole crowd."

She waited and I dutifully wrote down a few lines of nonsense.

"Aunt Gloria's husband…"

"Monty Doyle. A no-goodnik. Don't mention him in mixed company or you'll get funny looks. That plane crash was the best thing that ever happened to her. Monty, may he rest in peace, was worth more dead than alive. No big loss. Thanks to the insurance, she made out like a bandit and still had the rest of her life ahead of her." Phyllis's envy palpable.

"Why didn't Uncle Eugene ever get married?"

The question surprised her and it took her a few moments to frame a response. "I suppose…because he didn't meet the right person." Cocking her head. "And just for the record, Scoop, Gene and I never dated. We were strictly friends. And you're getting that straight from the source."

"Sure, sure." Blushing because she'd read my mind.

Slowly, by subterfuge and misdirection, I added to my learning. An education that involved lurking around corners, eavesdropping and decryption. Excellent qualifications for a teacher, writer…or a peeping tom.

I found my parents' attitude toward Eugene puzzling and mysterious but had to be tactful how I pursued my investigations, lest I arouse their suspicions. Also, talking about his dead sibling tended to anger and depress my father so I had to choose my spots carefully.

It's easy, in retrospect, to trace dad's decline to his brother's untimely death. I've heard my mother, a woman not prone to sentiment, opine on numerous occasions that it was like a light went out. Dad lost his zest for life. Bought the car dealership, moved out west and poured himself into building the business. The smoking and drinking increased and he made less time for leisure and relaxation. As adolescents, Connie and I rarely interacted with him.

We found out later there had been warning signs. Shortness of breath, chest pains, doctor's prohibitions. He never let on. Likely fooled himself right up until I found him on the floor of the garage. Dead at least an hour, sprawled on the cold cement, tools scattered around him.

He outlived his brother by less than five years.

Both deaths, in a way, self-inflicted.

Then the funeral and one last encounter with Jack Donahue. Perhaps the memory of that episode is the real impetus for my later investigations. The helplessness I felt in his presence, the dread he so effortlessly inspired.

Needing to understand a man who could wield such power and, also, the dark source from whence it sprang.

In the single volume of poetry I've published, *Beleaguered Spirits* (Sylvan Lake Press), there's a poem called "1977" that begins with the lines: *In 1977 Elvis died/& so did my father/while the world mourned a King/I wept for the man who never was…*

The rest of the poem doesn't live up to the opening but I think it's pretty clear dad's death came as an enormous psychic shock to me. So much of what comes afterward, the twists and turns of my life, is, in some way, a byproduct or side effect of finding his body that day. I'm convinced of it.

In the years following my father's death, I learned more about his secret life. Family weddings and funerals usually provided the backdrop, drink and the passage of years loosening tongues. I was old enough to hear the stories that had previously been withheld or bowdlerized. That's when my eyes were opened to dad's double existence, his job with the city of Kingston, like Eugene's, a mere cover. It turned out he was one of "the boys" too. And there was no handshake agreement between my grandfather and a trusting banker. The money for the farm was loaned to them at an exorbitant rate of interest by a certain nameless party operating out of Hamilton and my grandparents nearly broke their backs paying it off. Years of absolute hell and hardship before they finally turned the corner. They couldn't *wait* to get shed of the place.

It became evident that our family's underworld connections were even more tangled and extensive than I'd imagined, affiliations stretching back to the old country. Just because you took the Mick out of Ireland didn't necessarily mean you got the Ireland out of…and so on.

Understand, none of us flaunt our criminal ties or goes around bragging about them. It's just part of our identity, who we are. Not to be alluded to in the presence of strangers or outsiders.

I was twenty and working on a commerce degree (bored stiff and about to switch to education), when the other shoe dropped. I was reading a magazine article on organized crime and came across a passage describing the biggest challenge facing any significantly large illegal endeavor: disposing of the money. Elaborate strategies must be devised for laundering the huge profits derived from unlawful activities, including using various front companies to convert ill-gotten gains into cold, hard cash. Establishments like, for instance, restaurants, bars and (*ulp*) car dealerships.

I broke the news to Connie but, as usual, she was way ahead of me. "Bruz, sometimes I wonder about you."

"So you've suspected all along?" Lagging behind the bell curve, yet again.

"You're calling right in the middle of supper. I've got one kid banging her head on the table and my boobs are leaking because I'm overdue to feed the other leech—"

"So how deep are we in it? I mean," lowering my voice for some reason, "are we legit or not?"

She laughed. "You checked your birth certificate lately?"

"Don't evade the question."

"Look, dummy, you wanna spend the rest of your life beating yourself up over where that silver spoon in your mouth came from, be my guest. As far as I can see, we made out okay thanks to daddy's so-called 'connections'. Remember the big house, the pool? How about that university education you're getting? I know for a fact those summer jobs of yours didn't pay for all of it."

"Okay, Con. I get your point."

"Do you? I doubt it. I have a feeling this is going to eat away at you. That over-developed conscience of yours. But take my advice and don't try squeezing anything out of mom, you'll only end up getting your head ripped off. Believe me, I speak from experience."

"You asked *Phyllis* about it? Jesus, that took nerve. How long ago was that?"

"Not long enough." I could hear the shiver. "That woman can be downright vicious at times."

"You don't have to convince me. She always scared me more than dad. She was the real power behind the throne."

"That's the first smart thing you've said so far." She sighed. "Vonda just spilled her milk onto her plate. The whole glass. On *purpose*." Her tone murderous. "Gotta go." And just before the receiver slammed down: "*Why, you little…*"

# One

# School's Out (Forever)

C onnie was right: I didn't forget and I couldn't let it go.

But life continued and before I knew it, I'd finished university, found a teaching job in Saskatoon (literally within a month of convocating), settled down, married, fathered two sons, paid taxes, contributed to my community and so on. But in the back of my mind a stubborn, annoying voice insisted everything I had—my safe, comfortable circumstances, financial security (relatively) and good fortune—was somehow rotten and fetid at its roots.

It's my belief that *secrets*, not to mention the lies and rationalizations employed to conceal them, have had a corrosive effect on our family. My mother used dad's death as an excuse to sever nearly all of her social ties, divesting herself of friends and acquaintances with the same swift ruthlessness she displayed when selling off the dealership. Over the years Phyllis has withdrawn from the world to the extent that she is, at present, a virtual shut-in. I suppose it's a kind of self-imposed agoraphobia; she doesn't seem to mind her isolated existence or pine for regular human contact. A happy hermit.

Connie and Reg married right out of high school, which was a mistake. They started drifting after their first child was born and eventually it got so bad it was either go their separate ways or take out restraining orders on each other. She's had terrible luck in relationships and struggles constantly with loneliness. I try to keep in regular touch but thanks to the challenges of single parenthood, her life is even more hectic than mine. More often than not, we end up talking about our kids, only rarely venturing beyond that safe subject.

I recall a specific exchange that took place during one of our customary Christmas Eve phone calls. We were both somewhat tipsy. After the usual holiday season chit-chat, we got talking about dad, the perspective the passing years have given us.

Then, as if anticipating where this was undoubtedly heading: "It's not like he was Vito Corleone," she said.

"Uncle Eugene either. They were cogs in a machine. Interchangeable parts. Drones. Useful as long as they served their roles. They did a job and got paid for it, same as the rest of us."

"But who or what were they serving?"

"Supply and demand," she answered. "I believe they call it *capitalism*. Listen, every time you buy a tin of fruit from Latin America or a t-shirt made in some factory in Bangladesh, you're supporting a system of indentured servitude. Big business is just as crooked as the mob, bruz. Or haven't you been watching the news?"

That's my Connie. Always calling a spade a spade.

"But, Con, the man lied, made us believe—"

"I got news for you, dummy: everyone lies. If we went around telling the truth all the time, we'd end up killing each other. And when we don't lie, we cope. We get by. Making the necessary compromises to live as pain-free an existence as possible." I heard her drag on a cigarette. She keeps swearing she's giving them up. Bitching about her unhealthy lifestyle and shitty existence while firing up another cancer stick. What a gal. "You feel betrayed. Big deal. Get over it. We're all guilty, we're all complicit. Not a single one of us has a right to cast the first stone. And that includes you."

Sixteen months older and twenty lifetimes smarter.

Did my ruminations on our family's hidden history contribute to the anxieties that beset me throughout my teaching years, feelings of dread and self-loathing that threatened my peace of mind and, on a few occasions, played havoc with my sanity? Not sure I can answer that. Even now, so many years later.

To outward appearances I was a competent, highly organized teacher. Not very inspired or imaginative (hey, mostly I taught Canadian history, what do you expect?), but students came away with at least a fundamental understanding of the material and my classrooms were always well-structured and respectful learning environments. In what amounted to an inner city high school, those were considered *huge* positives.

But those anxious periods wouldn't go away. On the contrary, as time went by, they got worse and worse. I began self-medicating, mainly with alcohol and pot. Really, *really* bad days, I'd have to smoke a joint on the way to work, keeping the windows rolled down to dissipate the smell. My ruses and masks so effective no one—not my wife and sons, colleagues and students—suspected how awful and unbearable my life was becoming.

And then, after years of dodging and denying, keeping a bottle wrapped in a towel in my briefcase, a baggie of pot stashed in the garage, I couldn't do it any more. I'd start losing sleep in early August, just *thinking* about teaching again in the fall. Lie awake at night, my mind refusing to shut down, running these constant loops, a sea of expectant faces, trotting out the same lesson plans and quizzes year after year, the pointlessness of my efforts. For most kids, history isn't the problem, it's their current, present day crises and dramas that demand their undivided attention. History means it's already happened and, therefore, of no further interest. Out of date, like last month's calendar. *Yawn.* It's what's going to happen next that's important. What that twisted fucker Fate has in store just around the corner, *that's* what should be weighing heavily on your mind. Knowing it's something you'll never expect...

Finally, the toll got to me. Too many sleepless nights and joyless days. Behaving like a zombie at home because I was either tired, wired, drunk or stoned. I later discovered my wife and sons chalked my symptoms up to "exhaustion". They thought I worked too hard, cared too much about my students.

They never realized I was coming apart, unraveling at the seams like an old, frayed softball.

The thing about falling is that sooner or later you hit the ground. Rock bottom. Often, you never see it coming.

My last day as a teacher started the same as a thousand others. Hung over from a few too many nips of cheap, blended scotch the night before, dragging my ass but determined to soldier on. Got to work early that morning in order to commandeer the photocopier for a unit test on the Riel Rebellion. Thirty copies, collated and stapled (thankfully, the finicky machine was on its best behavior).

Went up to my classroom, briefcase in one hand, sheaf of test papers under my free arm. Unlocked the door, switched on the light. Walked over to my desk, set everything down. Surveyed the classroom in front of me, six rows of unoccupied desks, and thought *no fucking way*.

I'm not kidding. It was exactly like that: a switch flipped, a circuit closing.

Suddenly my throbbing hangover lifted and I realized I'd taken the first breath of what I assumed was freedom. I started shaking but couldn't pull out my chair, didn't want to sit behind that desk. Didn't want to be anywhere *near* it.

The mind is a funny thing, isn't it? It can absorb incredible amounts of punishment and abuse, endure heinous trauma, and then one day decide, *that's it, I've had enough, I am outta here*.

TILT.

And I want to emphasize, there was no premeditation, I had no idea when I drove to work that morning that I was going to be leaving my profession. Forever.

Charlie Dalrymple couldn't believe what he was hearing. "You're quitting? *Quitting*? As of right now?" I sat in a chair before his L-shaped desk, my hands squeezed between my knees. Still trembling. Keeping my composure, however, sounding perfectly reasonable and coherent as I explained that I no longer felt qualified to teach and intended to take an indefinite leave of absence.

Charlie was your prototypical principal, middle-aged, balding, an ex-athlete fighting a losing battle with flab. During staff meetings he referred to us as his "team" and spoke passionately about the power of positive thinking. Privately, he'd confided to me that he considered me one of his "star players" and bemoaned the lack of spirit he detected from other staff members, singling out the science guys for special mention.

Now he was exhorting me to "get back on the horse" and "go back in there and face down your demons" and similar rot. The kind of spiel that wouldn't cut the mustard with a roomful of high school football players, let alone a guy having a nervous breakdown.

I wouldn't be moved. I told him to arrange for a sub, mentioned the exam papers I'd left on my desk. Thanked him for his courtesy and consideration (!), rose to my feet and left. Didn't say good-bye to anybody or look back. Barely returned greetings to staff and students I encountered on the way out of the building and as I walked through the parking lot.

They were like ghosts to me.

Or was it the other around?

Initially, my wife had a hard time dealing with her husband's apparent intransigence. How in the name of God could I throw away a solid, secure job, with a good salary, pension and benefits (yes, let's not forget those benefits, including medical and dental, plus a decent eye care plan)? And what other occupation gave you nearly two months off every summer?

But I have to say for the most part she was quite patient and considerate toward me. She listened, asked questions, trying her utmost to grasp what I was going through. On a number of occasions she mentioned "mental fatigue" until I finally corrected that misapprehension.

"It's not like I'm tired or worn out...well, that's part of it, but it's more like I can't—fake it any more. I can't pull it off, be that guy at the front of the room, teaching dates and treaties, getting them to color in maps and shit. I don't believe in it...and I don't believe in *him*. And I don't want that to be my identity. Because it would only be a mask, nothing like my true face."

"So who are you then?" Hanging in there but mystified by my explanation.

"I don't know," I admitted. "But I want to find out."

We looked at each other.

"Are *we* welcome on this…journey of discovery of yours?" Meaning her and our sons.

"Of course," I said, not missing a beat, "couldn't do it without you."

Her shoulders sagged and she started crying, I mean, *sobbing*, like her heart was being wrenched out. I felt confused, stricken. You have to understand, my wife *never* cries. Not during sappy movies, not when she cuts her finger, not on our wedding day, *nada*. She once played an entire half of a university basketball game with a fractured wrist. A tomgirl and jock, six-one and tough as nails.

Not that day. She confessed afterward she was terrified of losing me, that I was having some kind of mid-life crisis and intended to abandon her and the boys and run off with some floozy or blow our savings on a Porsche, with personalized plates reading "2STUPID2LIVE".

I scooted closer to comfort her while she rallied herself. "It's not you," she said, blotting her eyes with the bottom of her shirt. "I just have to let go of *this*, what we had. I'll be okay…"

And, you know, she was. As a matter of fact, she was wonderful. The best partner a nervous wreck could hope for as he embarked on a new phase in his life.

The teachers' union arranged for counseling and our family doctor sold me on the benefits of anti-anxiety medication. I guess it helped me through the rough spots but I didn't keep it up long. Not a big fan of pharmaceutical companies and the poisons they peddle.

Mainly, I got better because I wasn't teaching. Without that stress in my life, the drinking dropped off to nothing and I ended up giving the remainder of my dope to one of my neighbors, a city cop on leave for PTSD. He needed it more than I did.

I'd been something of a runner back in the halcyon days of youth (*ahem*), nailing decent times in both the fifteen hundred and five thousand meter distances. Almost medaled at a city track meet but I cramped up on the last lap and couldn't hold my position. I always enjoyed pushing myself, that rush of endorphins as you forge on despite the pain, thighs and calves burning, your heart hammering in your chest. Now that I had time on my hands, I decided to give it another shot, digging out an old pair of sweats, starting modestly with a few circuits around the neighborhood. Initial results weren't encouraging (can you say *shin splints*?) but, masochist that I am, I stuck with it. Within a couple of months I was up to 5 k a day and feeling better than I had in *ages*. And I haven't looked back since. It's rare that I miss a day and when I do I always regret it.

I like to jog to music and over the years I've assembled a number of playlists, featuring tunes that would make my wife and sons howl in derision (they're hard core metalheads, especially the former, who often wears an Opeth tour shirt as a nightie). Looking for 45 minutes (or so) worth of music to run to? In my humble opinion, you could do a lot worse than my current favorite:

1. "Running Up That Hill" (Kate Bush)
2. "Running on Empty" (Jackson Brown)
3. "Runaway Train" (Soul Asylum)
4. "(I'm Gonna) Run Away" (Joan Jett)
5. "My Little Runaway" (Del Shannon)
6. "I Ran (So Far Away)" (Flock of Seagulls)
7. "Band on the Run" (Wings)
8. "You Can Run But You Can't Hide" (Solomon Burke)
9. "Run Like Hell" (Pink Floyd)
10. "Run, Run, Run" (Velvet Underground)
11. "On The Run" (K-OS)
12. Theme from "Rocky" (Bill Conti)

And so things were looking up. I was getting in shape, mentally and physically, my sleep cycle improving, my appetite better, my sex drive—well, to be honest, that's never been a problem. Before long, my wife and sons were commenting on how much brighter and more cheerful I seemed. My lads were still in grade school when I quit teaching and while they were surprised by my decision, they were not, it turned out, unduly alarmed.

"Whatever makes you happy, pop." That about summed up their feelings.

I don't deserve my family, I really don't.

And so, at thirty-seven years old, I found myself starting over again.

What would I do? What were my plans?

What I hadn't told anyone was that in the back of my mind, kept in a special, cordoned off area no one was permitted to visit, I had a notion of becoming a writer.

About five years into my teaching gig I came up with this character, a boy I dubbed *David Primeau*. David was a composite of a half dozen kids I'd run across in my class-room. He was *métis*, bright, witty, resourceful, courageous. But David faced many hurdles in his life: I envisioned a wayward, alcoholic father who'd occasionally show up and wreak havoc. I pictured a sister, fifteen years old, living at home, struggling with a new baby, their mother working hard to keep her family from imploding.

There were a lot of things conspiring against young David, but he was also a gifted athlete, excelling in a number of sports thanks to an indomitable heart. Because of his difficult home life, he had trouble focusing on academics, frequently plagued by his *bête noire*, a racist vice-principal who hated him and wanted to see him fail.

I conceived a cycle of stories, episodes that followed him right through high school. I made notes, outlined various characters and subplots during lunch hours or whenever I could grab a free moment. "A *Chocolate War* for aboriginal kids!" I scrawled across one page.

It showed *chutzpah* on my part, a certain amount of stupid confidence. *The Chocolate War* is a classic of young adult literature. You can't say I wasn't aiming my sights high.

After I'd ditched medication, taken up running and cleared out my system, I determined it was time to revisit my dream of becoming an author. I went into the little alcove off the living room I use as a home office and dug out my "David Primeau" file.

At first, I was reluctant to open it, worried my brilliant ideas weren't worth the sheets of foolscap paper they were scribbled on. Over the years, I'd added to the dossier — story notes, newspaper clippings on related issues—but it had been a significant period of time since I'd taken a good, hard look at the material.

I carried the file into the kitchen. Poured some coffee, stared at the folder. Deep breath and—

There were good bits but most of it was terrible. Nothing cohesive, just a number of unrelated scenes and vignettes, the timeline wandering all over the place. I was getting discouraged, losing faith in the whole thing…and that's when I came across the aforementioned sheet, the handwriting recognizably mine.

"A *Chocolate War* for aboriginal kids…"

I flipped the sheet over, picked up my pen and began to write.

*David Primeau gazed out the window, longing to be anywhere except inside an airless, stifling classroom…*

I was still at it when my family came home.

I think I can honestly say that's when my healing really began.


My *David Primeau* series performed well in the young adult marketplace. I'll be the first to admit it was mostly a matter of luck and good timing (i.e. schools were seeking more culturally sensitive reading and resource material and it didn't hurt having a *métis* kid for a protagonist, white establishment figures acting in opposition). Once the books made it on to the curriculum and schools started buying class sets, I did all right. The third installment was longlisted for a Caldecott, which delighted me to no end.

Writing those seven books was incredibly cathartic and while I'll never claim they achieve the status of high literature, I do think the stories are honestly and compellingly told. I know many young readers identify with David because a substantial number of them have sent me fan letters (some addressed to my fictional creation!).

A small production company in Winnipeg optioned the series and apparently there might be a TV show in the offing. In the meantime, income from sales helped pay off our mortgage and we were able to put a little aside for the kids' future, as well as add to our retirement nest egg.

But, oh, those taxes…

After nearly a decade I was finally ready to say a warm *sayonara* to David, allowing him to graduate and go on to (we hope) bigger and better things. Once the last book was delivered to my publisher, I didn't write any prose for months. Instead, I went through a period of reflection and self-examination that resulted in my *Beleaguered Spirits* collection. The one with "1977" and another poem where I refer to my father as "a quiet, amiable criminal/too good to be true".

I was surprised my mother missed the reference.
Or maybe she simply chose to ignore it.
With Phyllis, you never know.

## Two

# *The Lonesome Death of Ted Hoffman*

The way I heard it, the story went like this: One day during the summer of 1972, my uncle Eugene drove (or was driven) to a park near Kingston where, in the company of several other gentlemen of long association, he participated in the gangland style execution of a man named Theodore (Ted) Hoffman.

It was, by all accounts, a gruesome scene. Every manner of torture was devised by whoever was telling the tale, including the victim having his hands and feet nailed to a tree. Hoffman, it was alleged, had broken one of the cardinal rules and a message needed to be sent to the rank and file. The details varied wildly but let's just say that on one point all the narratives agree: it took the unfortunate Mr. Hoffman a long time to die. His captors undoubtedly well-versed in the art of inflicting agony.

I don't know what role Eugene played and refuse, at this point, to resort to conjecture. I'd like to think he took no active part in the proceedings, but for all I know he could have been the one meting out punishment, the worst of the bunch. I have a hard time believing that, it wouldn't fit with the man I remember. My father called him a 'failed saint' and though he never explained the reference, that image kind of stuck with me. My mother thought Eugene fell in with the wrong crowd at the wrong time. I recall him looking like a math teacher or accountant: thinning hair, beaky nose and a weak chin. No resemblance to any of the mobsters or Bad Guys I'd seen on TV or at the movies.

That said, he was there the day Ted Hoffman met his grisly end. But it must have bothered him, eaten away at him, how else do you explain what followed? Because within six weeks he was gone too. Only before he died, he must have told somebody, who told somebody else. Before long, it entered into family lore. The older gener-ation tactfully avoided the subject (it was considered poor taste to mention the incident directly or refer to the parties involved). However, among the younger crowd it became almost a standing joke, shared over an illicit cigarette or liquor nicked from our parents' private stock.

"Watch it, buster, or I'll send you to Camp Hoffman!"

That kind of thing.


My father's relationship with his dead brother continued to fascinate me. After dad died, I had few people to turn to in order to satisfy my curiosity. His sister Gloria lived in Kingston and didn't encourage regular contact. Which left my mother.

"What do you want to know about that stuff for?" She demanded when I pressed her for more information. "Forget about Gene. Likely got drunk, fell off the dock at Gananoque and drowned. Nothing mysterious about that."

"But I heard—"

"Never mind what you heard." Pointing her finger at me. "Don't be listening to those stories. People inventing crap, trying to impress each other. Nobody knows anything, they just *think* they do. I *hate* those people and that's why I couldn't wait to get out of Kingston. All the whispering and *pss pss pss.*"

I could see I wasn't going to make any headway the direct route so I decided to finesse her a little. "Dad said he was a 'failed saint'."

She had to look away. "He was too soft-hearted…"

"Uncle Eugene?"

"Your father!" Glaring at me. "And don't you *dare* bring any of this up with your Aunt Gloria."

"Does she know about it? Any of it?"

But my mother wouldn't answer. Her relations with Gloria were cordial but never close. Gloria the more sophisticated, a world traveler and symphony buff. Married some mobbed up guy who subsequently lost his life in a private plane crash (rumour had it he was a courier and over a million dollars burned up along with him in the wreck). Insurance left her a wealthy widow. Mom felt diminished in her company. We all did. Her big house outside Kingston. Huge and elegant, not a blade of grass or article of finery out of place. Afraid to touch anything or look at it the wrong way.

"'The proceeds o' crime'," my father called it once as we were driving away after a visit.

"What d'you mean?" I demanded from the back seat. Beside me, Connie sniggered.

"Never mind," he muttered, ducking his wife's evil eye.

"Then why'd you say it?"

"It was a slip of the tongue. Spoken in jest." Meanwhile, Phyllis's glare could've fried an egg.

See what I was dealing with? In our family, you had to read between the lines. Watch for patterns and congruencies, certain names recurring.

"Never should've hooked up with Jack Donahue…"

"…bloody Jack Donahue…

"…Donahue…"

I did, in fact, ask Aunt Gloria about our family history, several times. These were acts of desperation, really. Every other avenue closed to me.

It was worse than dealing with Phyllis, and that's saying something.

I mean, the old gal could've bent a *little*, offered up a story or two about her  beloved brothers but, no, every overture I made was either rebuffed or ignored. I wrote to her most recently a couple of years ago, making up some pretext to grill her about our family tree. Completely bogus, of course, but I played it safe by sticking to general questions, hedging when it came to the central theme: *where the hell do I come from?*

Her response was predictably cagey. In a brief note that arrived two months later (she'd been to Oberammergau, she explained, attending the *Passion Play*), she claimed (yet again) to know little about our family history and, furthermore, had scant interest in helping fill in the blanks. "What's relevant is what you do with your own life, not the unchangeable past," she wrote. "Although in terms of medical background I suppose you should know that our line seems prone to heart disease, poor circulation and early onset rheumatism. I hope that's helpful to you."

Yeah, thanks a lot, Aunt Gloria. About as helpful as a kick upside the head.

But she was only sticking to the party line: see no evil, speak no evil. It was a script my mother followed to perfection.

Time passed and, eventually, so did Gloria.

Then I was really stuck.

So what do you do when you want to find out something, some crucial bit of knowledge, but *no one* wants to talk to you or answer your questions?

Well, I don't know about you, but *I* call a newspaper…

\* \* \* \* \*

I figure Kingston's *Whig Standard* is the logical place to start, rather than the *Globe & Mail* or Toronto *Star*. The events in question, the people involved, part of their local beat (albeit a few decades removed). But when I ring them up and ask to speak to one of their crime reporters, there's a pause, after which I'm informed there's no longer any such animal. Which sort of throws me for a loop. What now? "Then…how about someone in your archive department—do newspapers still have 'morgues', like the old days?" The person I'm talking to hasn't the foggiest idea. She puts me on *Hold* for awhile and then I'm connected to someone in Editorial, who listens to the first part of my pitch before curtly suggesting I seek on-line sources for my 'personal inquiries', disconnecting before I can argue the point further.

I decide to take her advice, do some *Googling* and keep encountering the name *Neil Flory*. He sounds vaguely familiar—his modest *Wiki* page provides more details. He comes across as an old style, cigar-chewing newshound who specialized in stories relating to crime, organized or otherwise. He worked for six different newspapers in Ontario and the Tri-State region, winning numerous awards during a forty-year career. I picture him in a rumpled, off the rack suit and porkpie hat, a familiar character haunting local courtrooms and police precincts like a persistent ghost. Chewing a stogie and firing one-liners and sharp-tongued witticisms right and left. Forced into retirement by downsizing and his cantankerous disposition, an inability to hold his nose in an era of corporate-sponsored news.

These days you can find anything with a few clicks of the mouse, so it's only a matter of minutes before I have contact information, including an e-mail address. No indication that he's deceased.

Nope, not dead, it turns out, very much alive. Not only that, but bored and eager to talk about the good, old days. All it takes is a short email, the briefest outline of my situation. He takes over from there:

*Great to hear from you and, yes, indeed, I'm familiar with most if not all of the names you've listed!*

*I don't think I met your father or uncle but I certainly know who they were. They were two of Jack Donahue's lads. Mr. Donahue is, of course, currently resting in peace in our local cemetery. His soul, I imagine, inhabiting somewhat warmer climes. Many of the lads from that era no longer reside this side of heaven. A good number made early departures. Including your uncle and father, by the sound of it.*

*One always hears stories in my line of work and Eugene's "suicide" always seemed very convenient to me. There was a lot of upheaval in mob circles at that time, everyone turning informant, ratting on each other in return for immunity from prosecution. A number of supposedly hard men I was acquainted with escaped long prison sentences, even death row, by turning state's evidence.*

*When push comes to shove, self-interest wins out over any of that "omerta" stuff any day.*

*Things have changed and "the boys" don't carry the weight they used to (at least publicly...plenty still going on behind closed doors). Back in the day, Jack Donahue's name meant something. He made good copy and he wasn't a total thug like that Bulger guy in Boston. Mick gangster, part of the "401 Gang" (named after the highway, I'm sure you've heard of it, our version of the autobahn). Jack was a real charmer, which isn't to say he wasn't capable of brutality if the situation demanded it. You mentioned the story of Ted Hoffman and, I assure you, that's merely the tip of the iceberg.*

*I'm retired now but still have most of my marbles. I kept tons of files and they contain a treasure trove of information for someone like you. It's at your disposal. If you can provide me with specific questions, dates, that would be helpful. And if you're ever in the neighborhood, feel free to drop by and pick my brain...*

We were at home in Kingston when they found Eugene. Gloria called and she was a mess. Keening his name over and over. For some reason the police notified her first. She didn't know what to do, needed help, someone to shoulder the burden...

My dad hung up, turned to my mother. "He's dead." He didn't notice me yet. "They found the body and she says they need someone to…" His face flushed, leaning against the nearest wall for support. "They aren't saying, they haven't said yet…" Hitching in his breath. "But *I* know. We *both* know who's responsible."

My mother went over, grabbed his arm. "Terry? Terry, listen to me: *what did Gloria tell you?*" He started to answer but some instinct made him aware of my presence. My mother spotted me, waved me away. As I left, I heard her hiss: "Fucking Jack Donahue…"

I can't recall why I went looking for him. Asking permission for something or, more likely, after money.

Our attached garage the last place left.

My father's face. An image I'll never, *ever* forget. Turned toward me, swollen, mottled with broken blood vessels, almost unrecognizable.

Contorted by the agonies of an exploded heart.

I couldn't bring myself to touch him, knew he was beyond help. I stood there and part of me was aware I had to tell someone about this, but another part resisted. What it came down to was that I was reluctant to leave him alone. I couldn't make myself approach him, nor could I back away. I don't know how long I was rooted there. I don't remember what I was thinking. That part is a total blank. I suppose I was grieving. But if so, where were the tears?

"Hey, there, kiddo, how you doin'? I'm your Uncle Jack…"

My father's funeral, January, 1977. Two brothers dying so young and less than five years apart. So much for the luck o' the Irish.

Back at the family home in Parkridge after a typically tepid United Church service and speedy interment (it was winter in Saskatchewan, after all). Coats piled three deep on the downstairs guest bed. You couldn't get past the boots and shoes by the front door. The mat and nearby floor soaked from melting snow. I was in the kitchen, fetching some cold chicken from the fridge. Turned around and there he was.

My mother pointed him out at the cemetery. He stood apart from the others, not a big man but possessing a quality that drew your eye, singled him out as a person of significance. Another thing that impressed me was he kept his head uncovered through the entire graveside service. And it was *cold* that day. "Lord, that man has nerve to show up today, of all days."

"Maybe he wants to pay his respects."

That answer didn't sit well with my mother. She was in a foul mood, cranky, exhausted and ungenerous. "Bloody Jack Donahue. The *bastard*. Make sure you steer well clear of him."

"…I'm your Uncle Jack. Youse remember me?"

"Sure, Mr. Donahue." We shook hands. "My mother and I were surprised you came. Glad, obviously, but—"

He didn't let go of my hand. "Surprised, were you?" Smiling, no indication of anger or displeasure. *But he wouldn't relinquish his grip.* "Now why would you say that then?"

I struggled to act nonchalant. "Well, it's just that it's—it's such a long way to come. You know…" My alarm ramping up close to panic.

"Sure I know. Know your whole family, kiddo. Longer than you've been alive. Family is everything, least where I come from." He kept up the pressure, refusing to release me until he was satisfied he'd made his point. "Know what I mean?"

"I—I think so. Yeah." I just wanted my damn hand back. Finally, he relented.

"That's good. Youse remember that. It's an important lesson." There was a trace of brogue. My father got it too, usually after a few drinks. "And you mind your mother, hear? See that you take some o' the load off. You're old enough, practically a grown man, ain't that right?"

"Yeah…" I muttered. Trying to edge away, cowed and spooked by whatever it was he was giving off. He stayed close, speaking directly into my ear.

"If there's a problem, you call me. We offered to help with the funeral but she's a proud woman. Here." Pressing a wad of hundred dollar bills into my hand. "You wait and give her this later. Tell her we took up a collection. You got that?"

"Yeah."

"Hey…" Something in his voice made me look up. "Listen when I'm talkin' to you. You say youse was surprised to see me. That's good. 'Cause you never know with me, when I'm gonna turn up. I'm like one o' those bad pennies." Tapping the side of his nose. "Best keep that in mind, lad. Just…store it away in that noggin o' yours. For safekeeping, like."

With that, he disappeared in a puff of smoke.

Well. Just about.

Dad had just turned forty-eight.

Pretty much the same age I am now.

Sobering? Oh, yeah.

And now, as of earlier this year, Gloria's gone. The last of my father's siblings.

She outlived them all, achieving the ripe old age of seventy-seven. Quite the display of longevity, at least in our family. Ornery right to the end, even leaving special instructions in her will forbidding any kind of memorial service. She didn't want people crying over her or visiting her grave with handfuls of dead flowers. No empty gestures for our Gloria.

"I know you've always been curious about our family history," she wrote in one of her final letters. Crooked, shaky handwriting, on account of her arthritis. "Please believe me when I tell you that some memories are too painful and poisonous and little can be gained by bringing them to light. I have nothing to pass on to you and nothing else to add. My two brothers are dead and it won't be long before I join them. To be perfectly honest, I can hardly wait..."

*Mr. Flory:*

*Thanks for the speedy reply. Sounds like I'm talking to the right man!*

*I'm very interested in learning more about my family's lengthy association with Jack Donahue and his various underworld connections. This is purely for my own interest, at least for the moment, and I would certainly welcome any assistance or insight you might be able to provide.*

*I'll be in touch again soon. Until then, prepare yourself for a barrage of questions.*

*Best wishes,*

*etc.*

## "*They call me the Seeker...*"

**W**hat's this?

A text from my sister Connie down in Regina that begins: "Love that old lady!!!"

I read her message through once, then go back to the beginning and start over again. Hardly daring believe my eyes. I even call her in case it's some kind of joke.

"Bruz, I'm booking my ticket to Mazatlan as soon as the check clears…"

And it's weird how these things happen because all at once I know *exactly* what I'm going to do and with hardly a second thought set to work putting my plans into effect.

Which is totally weird and irrational behavior on my part (usually I'm the epitome of practicality). It's almost like I'm operating under a spell, like I've been *waiting* for this and now automatic processes are taking over.

By the time I talk to my wife that night, it's a done deal. *Fait accompli*. At least, as far as I'm concerned.

"So you're going to take this money—"

"*Some* of the money," I hasten to correct her. "I'll be working on a very tight budget." I've already drawn it up, I can show it to her if she asks. "I'll use Air Miles, get the cheapest flights I can, stay in dives if I have to. Whatever it takes."

"Sounds like you've given this a lot of thought." She's a remarkable woman, all too aware that she could squash this mad scheme of mine with a few deflating remarks. But I know she won't, that's the thing. We *could* use the bequest from my aunt to pay down our line of credit or stick it into RRSPs, salting it away for a rainy day. Which would be the smart thing to do and normally I'd be all for it. But not this time.

"It's just that I'm not sure I'm ever going to get another crack at it. Almost everyone who knew about this stuff, the ones that were actually there, are gone. Soon there won't be anybody left. And then I'll never know."

"Know what, exactly?"

"The world my father and uncle operated in. The way they *really* lived, not just the phony jobs and cover stories. What led to me finding him in the garage that day? I know the effect but...what was the cause?"

"But you said it yourself, these things happened so long ago, is there much chance of finding out anything new?"

"Neil thinks we'll be able to turn something up."

She gives me one of those *Oh, brother* smiles. She knows all about Neil. "I think it's great that you'll have a guide —"

"Not only that," I protest, "the entire area was his beat and he's familiar with everyone involved. This guy literally knows where the bodies are buried."

"He's also retired and lonely and e-mails you at least five times a day with suggestions and ideas and recipes..." We both chuckle because it's true. My query letter has given him a new lease on life and he's thrilled to be sharing the benefits of his years of experience and stored up gossip. "Listen," she says, reaching out and taking my hand, "I know this has been weighing on you for a long time. The way I look at it, this money from your aunt is like pennies from heaven. If you think you can put it to good use and finally get some peace of mind, I say go for it."

See? Absolutely fantastic. Not a word about the needless expense, the futility of the gesture. "Maybe I'll get a book out of it," I joke.

"Wouldn't that be nice?" Playing along.

"Except I don't do non-fiction," I remind her.

"Right," she affirms.

"No interest in a memoir."

"You're far too young anyway." Pause. "So have you told Tony about any of this? Assuming that you are, in fact, lying and are secretly plotting a new book project."

"I e-mailed him," I confirm, blushing right down to my bone marrow. "What he *really* wants is another series. He thinks it'll be easier to pitch. And to stick with the young adult stuff, maybe something with a harder edge, like Darren Shan."

She rolls her eyes. "The consummate agent and money-grubber. What he's *not* saying is he can get more for a multi-book deal, fifteen per cent of which goes directly into his pocket."

"You are a truly cynical person."

"And? So? What did he have to say about you rattling around in the family closet?"

I shrug. "He said to start with a magazine article. Think in terms of four or five thousand words and then maybe expand it from there."

"And does he think it could be…marketable?"

"He wasn't overly blown away. We're not talking about the *Sopranos*, just a bunch of small time hoods and racketeers."

"And murderers," she adds. "Remember that guy in the park you told me about, the one they tortured." And then finally revealing some misgivings. "None of those people are still alive, the ones who did that. You know that for certain, right?"

"It's not a business that encourages long life spans."

"So they're definitely pushing up daisies," she repeats, somewhat more forcefully.

"That or wilting away in retirement homes. Like you said, this stuff happened ages ago. No one cares any more. Ancient history."

Which seems to satisfy her. As well it should.

After all, that's the intention of my little, white lie.


It's a four-hour flight from Saskatoon to Ottawa, with an hour layover before I board a propeller-driven aircraft for the final leg to Kingston. It's the only part of the trip that makes me nervous. Putting my life in the hands of some rattletrap crate maintained and operated by a regional airline scraping by on a wafer thin margin. Is this going be one of those instances where curiosity really does kill the cat?

But, you know, everything goes swimmingly. During the flight to Ottawa, I drink some piss-warm Canadian *Chardonnay* and mostly stare out the window, trying to catch glimpses of our big country from thirty thousand feet. Feeling fortunate because my seatmate stays deeply engrossed in his laptop the entire trip. Hard at work on some sort of presentation that has to do with changing realities in the oil patch, bless his black, polluted heart.

I'm only allowing myself five days in Kingston— Monday to Friday—so I don't have any time to squander. I'll be relying heavily on Neil and that's a bit worrisome because I know he has health issues. He finally came clean in an e-mail he dubbed "Old men and their many afflictions":

*…I'm a diabetic, like I already told you, and don't get around that great. Lousy eyes, lousy circulation, painful piles and chronic dandruff. Why doesn't somebody shoot me and get it over with? I don't have a car any more so I'm afraid you'll have to rent one (not cheap, I know). None of this, needless to say, affects my mind or my memory, just another way of Nature telling me I'm getting old (and haven't taken proper care of the component parts). I still feel I can be an invaluable resource to you, even if I have to squint like Mr. Magoo to see and need to whiz about five times an hour…*

My assigned rental is a boxy new version of the Dodge Charger. Not much like the Chargers I remember from youth and where's that throaty rumble of old? The dashboard is a nightmare of digital displays and readouts and it comes equipped with *OnStar* in case I wander off course. A twenty-first century version of a muscle car. As phony as a three dollar bill.

I search out the bed and breakfast I'll be staying at during my sojourn in "the Limestone City" (God knows, we never called it that when I was growing up here). It's located in a quiet, tree-lined neighbourhood, not far from McBurney Park. I go inside and introduce myself to the owners/proprietors—the Warburtons, Kim and Henry— inspect my accommodations. Their establishment is a heritage home, over a hundred years old, three complete stories with an outside staircase. I'll have my own sepa- rate entrance and key, so I can come and go as I please. Overnight guests cost extra. Not a problem.

Then it's off to Gananoque to meet Neil. Initially, I thought about finding a B & B there but I know Kingston, or used to, plus it's centrally located, the nexus of many of the events I'll be looking into. I take #2, heading east. The highway skirts Lake Ontario so it's a scenic drive, rendered even more enjoyable by the classic rock booming from my speakers. Rolling Stones, The Kinks, Cream. Stuff that would make my family gag. Long, jagged lines of consecutive breakers off to my right—it's a treacherous lake, with its share of sunken ships and entombed men.

I call from my cell and when I roll up, Neil is waiting in front of his building. Short and wide, with old-fashioned, black-rimmed glasses, golf shirt and Chinos. Cheap rubber flip-flops complete the ensemble. "I'm retired," he announces when I step out to greet him, "I'm allowed to look like shit."

He leads me inside and I follow him down some stairs to the basement level, where each tenant has been assigned a small storeroom. Luckily, he knows which boxes and plastic bins are which and before long we've sorted things out. I have to make two trips and there's no elevator so I get a good workout in the process.

His third floor apartment is small and I can tell he's made an effort to clean up. It smells of ammonia and lemon-scented cleanser. The windows are open and despite the proximity of adjacent apartment blocks, some light manages to insinuate its way inside. The furniture is old, out of date, bumped and scraped from use. Some pictures and plaques, awards and citations for excellence in journalism. Everything in need of a good dusting.

We commandeer the kitchen table. He yanks open boxes and containers, gropes through the contents until he finds something worthwhile, tosses it aside. In no time at all, he's made an impressive stack. Another box contains his reporter's notebooks, long and thin, bound together with rubber bands, every one of them numbered and dated, some going back to the early 1960's.

"I'm a dinosaur," he confesses, "shoot, I even remember life without computers."

"And?" I prompt.

"It was easier," he admits.

He wasn't kidding, it's a veritable goldmine of material. Jack Donahue warrants his own file, clippings and photographs and copies of documents relating to various police investigations, court appearances, etc.

"Did you ever get to interview him? In person?"

Neil looks wistful. "Never had the pleasure, if you could call it that. He wasn't what you would call media friendly. Not like Capone or Gotti, some of those other guys. Most reporters were scared of him." He thinks about it. "I guess I was too."

"I can understand that. The last time I saw him was at my dad's funeral. He really put the fear of God into me."

"Did he have one of the boys with him? Dennis would be gone by then but…Mick Sloane maybe? Looked like a boxer, bent nose, face like a busted melon?"

"I know who you mean. I never saw Mick or any of the others. I'm pretty sure I would've recognized them."

Neil is dubious. "The man wouldn't come alone. Not even to a funeral." I try to recollect but no one comes to mind. "Someone would be there, minding the store."

"It was a cold day. Wind chill nearly thirty below."

Nodding. "Ah, that explains it. Probably keeping the car warm."

"Donahue kept his head uncovered through the entire graveside service."

"Did he now? Well, they went, back, didn't they? The brothers and him."

"That's what I'm here to find out. The extent of that involvement."

"Your father and his brother, uh—"

"Eugene."

"Right, okay..." He shifts uncomfortably. "Here's the thing. Your father and Eugene, well, they weren't what you would call bigshots, at least compared to some of the others. The equivalent of street bosses, so, y'know, a cut above the gorillas, but as far as your book goes, maybe not the most exciting stuff."

"Right now, this is more of a...personal quest. Who knows if it'll turn into anything—" I'm distracted by a clipping I've just spotted, *Body in Troy Area Accident Identified*. Dating from September, 1997.

*State Police have positively identified the occupant of a vehicle involved in a head on collision with a tractor-trailer on highway 481, five miles east of Troy...*

"The man makes it through all kinds of close scrapes and near misses, mostly avoids jail, definitely avoids responsibility for his many, many crimes." I look up as Neil chuckles. "And after all that, he ends up dying in a stupid car wreck. Guy in the semi dozed off, drifted around a curve into the oncoming lane and Jack, well, Jack was a speed demon, collected tickets like postage stamps. Not much left afterward."

"Was he alone?"

"So it seems." I give him a sideways look. "Yeah, " he acknowledges, "yet another mystery. What was he up to that he didn't want anyone with him?"

*...reputed underworld figure Jack Nathan Donahue, 71, a Kingston area businessman facing numerous racke-teering charges and recently acquitted in a trial involving influence peddling and corruption of public officials...*

"Sounds like they were finally closing in on him. Wonder if he could feel the heat."

"Donahue? Nah," Neil dismisses the notion. "He was a thick-headed, Mick bullyboy. Wore nice clothes and drank single malt whiskey but still a mug at heart. His kind always think they're going to get off. It's the nature of the beast to live in complete denial. No one wants to face up to the fact that they're either bound for jail or an early grave. Most likely one they've dug themselves." He excuses himself to use the facilities. Tells me to get used to it. "Overactive bladders, tricky tickers and irritable bowels," he mutters, shuffling away. "It sure ain't fun gettin' old, kid." Thanks to his poor circulation, his feet and ankles swell. He wears the flip-flops because most of the time his shoes won't fit. Poor bugger. Moved here after his retirement to be closer to his daughter by his first marriage and she turns around and hooks up with a guy from Qatar. She sends him e-mails and postcards, matter of factly informing him it frequently reaches 50° Celsius over there. Everything not air-conditioned intolerably hot to the touch. *It's like Hell, Pops, except there's no booze or Republicans...*

I dig out my binder, go through my notes. Cognizant of how Neil's mind tends to meander off topic, I've assembled several pages of questions, leaving room underneath to scribble his replies. I also brought along a digital recorder, in case it comes in handy. I'll probably avoid using it, I really hate transcribing.

Neil may think the brothers' lives lack the drama and significance that make for good storytelling but I'm not so certain. Besides, this isn't *Crime and Punishment* or "The Wire" and I'm not seeking a perfect story arc, with closure at the end. What I *hope* to come away with is a clearer understanding of my father and Eugene, the forces and key incidents that shaped and motivated them. What caused such radically different men to consciously choose a life of crime? If some of the whispers I've been hearing all my life are true, our little clan was involved with shady dealings going back to the old country: paramilitary actions, sanctioned hits, sectarian blood-letting.

This is the stock I come from. Violent, thin-skinned, blue-eyed people capable of terrible things. Ingrained from birth to fight, never back down or give an inch, but also never overlook the opportunity for a good chuckle, especially if it's at their own expense. A baffling and brilliant race. Someone once said that to be Irish is to know that in the end the world will break your heart. Freud remarked (in obvious exasperation) that they were the only people who couldn't be helped by psychoanalysis.

Those are my ancestral roots. My blighted family tree.

Which begs the question: what does that say about *me*?

While there's tons of material on Jack Donahue, my father and uncle aren't nearly as well represented.

"You have to understand," Neil pleads his case, "these kind of guys don't *want* to be in the limelight. They hate having their pictures taken or talking shop. They don't wanna be seen talking to a reporter—something like that is liable to get you killed. As long as they keep a low profile, nobody knows what they're up to." He picks up one of the notebooks. "There are bits and pieces. See?" Showing me a citation:

*Eugene (Gene) B. (see: Terry B.)—20s/local*
*check priors (call Wilmer/Klassen?)*
*Sweeney'sàK/A Miles Coughlin; Michael Sloane*
*G heavy bettor/sports/GGs*

"I know there's more," sorting through the stack. "It'll take time to go through it all."

"But you don't think there's much."

"If they associated with the likes of Mickey Sloane, they were hardly choir boys. That much is certain."

"I only saw Mick a few times. Didn't like being around him."

"You have good instincts." Closing the notebook, setting it aside.

"So he was as bad as he looked?"

"Let's just say he was a good man to have around when things got out of hand. Not so good if you were on the other side."

"Is he still alive?"

"Oh, sure. If you call doing life in Kingston Pen any kind of existence. Only now I hear they're thinking about closing the old place down so I guess they'll be moving him. I'm sure he'll be pining for sunnier pastures but if I was him, I wouldn't get my hopes up."

"He'll never get out?"

"For whacking two guys? And more they couldn't pin on him but knew he did. The Mickster doesn't stand a chance. One of the few not to turn rat. A truly hard man. So he got the maximum sentence, with all the side benefits." Shaking his head. "I'll tell you one thing, kid: if you were writing a book on Mickey Sloane instead of those brothers of yours, you'd have a helluva lot more stories to tell…"

Late afternoon, we take a break. We're both hungry and need fresh air. Three blocks from the building he asks: "So d'you think you'd be here if your aunt hadn't conked off?"

"Probably not." Slowing, pulling in behind a short line of vehicles waiting at a stop sign. "When my sister told me Gloria left us money, I was genuinely surprised.

There wasn't a lot of contact, especially after my dad died. Occasional notes and Christmas cards. It never occurred to me that she'd include me in her will. I wonder…"

"What?"

I glance at him. "If she suspected what I'd use the money for. Y'know, when she made me a beneficiary. I always got the impression she was one smart cookie."

"But you said she didn't like talking about family stuff."

"Not while she was alive, no. She'd shut it right down. Asking her about my father or Eugene was the equivalent of farting in front of the Queen." I turn left at the intersection, feeling comfortable and at ease, one hand on the steering wheel. "Her brothers' deaths must have affected her deeply. Losing Eugene devastated my father—maybe even killed him. All that boozing after hours, two packs of smokes a day for rocket fuel…I think he stopped caring whether he lived or died."

It's quiet for awhile. Then he says: "I know a place in town that serves the best seafood around." Adding: "And it's not far from the dock where, y'know…"

"Then that's where we're heading." Gananoque is an easy city to drive in: nobody speeds, everybody obeys traffic and pedestrian rules and the streets are clean and kept in good condition. A nice, neat community, sleepy and civic-minded. Neil provides excellent directions and before long we're pulling into the parking lot of *Pier 13*. You can smell the menu from outside.

And, as an added bonus, our waitress is pretty too…

The food is delicious but I basically bolt it down. Limit myself to one glass of wine, skip dessert and *still* end up shelling out over seventy bucks for our meal, including the tip. I sort of hurry Neil along, anxious to get there before it's too dark to see anything. But he points the way and soon we've found what we're seeking. This stretch of shore is west of the marina and it's been incorporated into a walking path that encircles the town. There's a fancy inn and spa nearby, deck chairs placed at intervals along a cement pad. Just ahead of us, to our right, a wooden dock juts out into the lake.

This is it. The exact spot where it happened, where my uncle came to his untimely end, accidentally or due to foul play.

Neil waits in the car (claiming his feet are killing him) while I walk out to the end of the pier. I stand there, listening to the waves slap against the pilings, trying to recreate or visualize…what? A dying man's last thoughts. Terror or capitulation? Did it matter once the water closed over him?

I confess I don't achieve any great insights or epiphanies. Who can say what goes through someone's mind when they're confronted with their own mortality? That's not something anyone else can even *guess* at. Was there somebody around who witnessed what happened? What was the last thing he heard or smelled or tasted? I meditate awhile, then head back to the car.

"Seen enough?" Neil asks and I nod. "Probably been a long day for you, huh? What with flying and all."

I stare straight ahead. Gazing at the out-thrusting dock, the wide, deep lake beyond.

*…we both know who's responsible…*

*…fucking Jack Donahue…*

Here. It happened right here.

But what fateful decisions or set of circumstances brought Eugene to this place? Was it suicide or murder? Did he jump or was he pushed?

## *Digging in the Dirt*

y morning is free because Neil has a doctor's appointment. "We're trying to figure out why my system's so out of whack. I get dizzy, lose my breath, the whole nine yards. Can't be my heart because I know for a fact I don't have one. Come and get me after lunch. We'll go on the prowl together."

I can tell he's relishing the notion. On the other hand, it's good to be on my own for a few hours and I intend to use that time do a little sniffing around on the sly.

Right after I deal with a couple of personal matters:

*Hey dad*, writes my oldest, *how goes yr research? Find out anything interesting yet? Pls tell me we're related to Bill Gates  : )*

*Dear son*, I text, *if I had more time and money I'd do this right, trace our family history all the way back to the Emerald Isle. We have a mean streak that runs through us like an ugly gene, stretching across oceans. Our enemies fear us and our friends don't much like us either...*

There are two messages from my wife, general inquiries and inconsequential updates. I call her from a bench in Kingston's Waterfront Park. It's a lovely morning, already in the mid-twenties, and there are quite a few people about, strolling, jogging, enjoying the view. There's a moderate offshore breeze and I can see the grey outline of a huge ship off in the distance and, closer in, two teenagers taking their first crack at kayaking, with predictably comic results.

"Your notes are worryingly banal," I say when she answers.

"Only geeky writers talk that way," she fires back.

"Guilty as charged."

"And, so, what are you up to? Find a good place to run yet?"

"Lots of people jogging around here. Nice view too, maybe I'll come back later. Last night I did five k around the park near my B & B."

"Music?"

I hesitate, knowing what comes next. "The Stone Roses."

"You're a sick, sick man."

"How the hell am I supposed to jog to Lamb of God? It's *impossible*, woman! I'd end up having a coronary."

"Pussy."

We're both laughing. People in the vicinity are glancing at me. "Let's change the subject, I'm getting funny stares."

"What's on for today?"

"Neil's seeing his doctor so I've got the morning to myself. Any suggestions?"

"You *could* visit with family. You said you still know people out there. Cousins and—"

"Nobody I'm really close to—and no one who'd approve of why I'm here."

"All right, so take in the local scene, do something touristy."

"Been there, done that. I grew up around these parts, remember? When I was a wee lad we did all that fun stuff: Fort Henry, the Thousand Islands cruise, Upper Canada Village, you name it. Don't imagine it's changed much."

"There's an actual *cruise*?"

"A big, double-decker liner weaves through the islands around here and you even get to stop at this for real castle to stretch your legs. And buy cheesy souvenirs, of course."

"Wouldn't be any fun unless I was there."

"True," I concede. "Besides, I think it's a day trip." We keep it up for awhile, then start to wind things down.

"No sign of men with bent noses lurking around outside your B & B?" she asks suddenly.

"Not so far, no."

"But you're being careful."

I'm surprised by her caution. "Darlin', it's been nearly forty years. This is a cold case if there ever was one."

"Wasn't it you who said there's no statute of limitations on murder?"

"Me and my big mouth."

"So watch yourself."

"Yes, ma'am."

"I'm *serious*."

I wait a decent interval, make sure I sound suitably solemn. "Okay."

Then we're fine.

The central library downtown doesn't open until ten so I take the Charger on a tour of my old haunts, retracing the route I used to walk to school. While the streets have the same names, the intervening four decades have taken their toll: the elementary school I attended is gone and condo developments are going up all over the place. I even cruise past 26 Clarence Street, just to have a look. No longer HQ of a criminal organization, currently home to a number of much more conventional enterprises including, on its main floor, a health food store and seniors drop-in centre.

My, how times have changed.

It's a newer building, probably built in the Fifties. Ugly. Steel and glass, standing out in area that features some truly beautiful architecture, including the nearby Prince George Hotel.

Maybe it's only my jaded point of view but I think Kingston lacks a *soul*. It's always been a really *white* city, if you know what I mean, not a whole lot of racial diversity. Affluent, conservative and, I'm starting to realize, more than a little on the boring side. The waterfront is getting cluttered with stupid high rises, just like Toronto — functional quadrilaterals, tall and straight and uniformly uniform. There's an underlying reserve and stodginess to the place, and it comes as no surprise when you learn it was once a haven for royalists escaping persecution during and after the American Revolution. Almost since inception its local economy was bolstered by a large military presence and, of course, the infamous penitentiary has been around since 1835.

I tool through the business district, admiring the gorgeous, Victorian-era buildings on Brock and Princess, locally quarried limestone and red brick predominating. Many of the structures at least a hundred and fifty years old.

I take a crack at finding Gloria's acreage north of the city, but take a wrong turn off some new bypass, ending up *miles* from where I want to be. Maddening. I beat a hasty retreat, manage to make it back downtown, park the Charger, buy an over-priced coffee from a café run by old hippies and loiter on a nearby bench until a few minutes past ten.

The central library on Johnson Street is an impressive structure, situated not far from city hall and St. George's Cathedral. It covers an entire block, circular in design, downright curvy, with lots of windows and a warm, friendly ambiance. I've hung around libraries since I was old enough to discover they let you take out books for *free* and retain my childhood affection and respect for the people who work in those hallowed halls. In my experience, they rarely let you down.

Happily, my luck holds true and the staff turn out to be first-rate. They direct me to the proper section and help identify promising titles. I fill them in on what I'm up to, which seems to pique their interest. One of the librarians grabs a volunteer page and the two of them scuttle off to do some independent searching, bringing me suggestions for other titles, which I duly note.

My best bet seems to be *Organized Crime in Ontario and Quebec* by George L. Poldark. Looks fairly recent and quite exhaustive. Not currently available, of course, but I can procure it *via* interlibrary loan when I get home or pick up a copy through Abebooks for a song. There are back issues of the region's newspapers I can plow my way through, if I'm so inclined, much of it on microfilm, still waiting to be digitized. Maybe if I was somehow granted a longer life span and this crazy obsession of mine had an ounce of practical value to anyone other than me...

This is a lark, I keep telling myself, nothing will come of it except I might fill in a few holes, learn a bit more about my family's checkered past. In the end, Eugene, my father and Gloria will be just as dead, just as unaccountable.

"Excuse me." It's Donna, the resource gal. East Coast accent, exhibiting the geniality and humour I associate with that region. "One of our staff remembered this one. It was in the process of being repaired but if you handle it carefully..."

In format, it resembles a scrapbook. Lots of pictures, some of them pretty gory. It reminds me of the issues of

*Argosy* I used to devour when I was a kid. *The Water Was Red: Fifty Years of Murder and Mayhem on the Great Lakes*, by Frank Lassiter.

"This looks terrific. Thanks." Adding it to the pile. "You folks have been great. This is much more than I expected." For the next couple of hours, I immerse myself in local lore. Good background for if/when this pet project of mine coalesces into something more substantial.

Kingston is an old city, this region rich in history. Battles, uprisings, invasions — it occupies a strategic position on the Canadian side of Lake Ontario, at the mouth of the St. Lawrence River, offering a tempting target to marauders, malcontents and those of a criminal persuasion.

There has always been smuggling and illegal trafficking back and forth on the Great Lakes, the cargos of choice ranging from booze, guns, and, most recently, cigarettes. Smokers want to die as cheaply as they can. And where there's illegal activity, there's organized crime. Groups of men working in concert to frustrate the system and escape with the spoils. Ruthlessly defending their turf, raking in the loot and never mind the human cost.

Since the 1940s, various Irish mobs have called the shots in these parts, their ambition and enterprise not confined by geographical borders or informed by ordinary scruples. Vice remains their primary source of income—gambling, contraband, chop shops, prostitution, drugs, etc.—but their tentacles reach much further. They've insinuated their way into positions of power and influence, used their bulging purses to buy political access and protection. While there are occasional efforts to expose them, weed them out, for the most part it's business as usual; sin, after all, never sleeps, never takes a holiday.

The ringleaders included men like Big Frank Turner, Ned Shelton, John Pearce and the Dwyer brothers. Seizing the reins of power, behaving like minor potentates, employing any means at their disposal to instill fear and intimidation. I find old black and white photos, figures lying in pools of blood beside bullet-riddled cars or sprawled ignominiously under tables in restaurants. Cops on the scene not bothering to cover the bodies for the sake of decency, photographers snapping away. Dimestore Weegees, undaunted by puddled gore and splattered brains.

The Lassiter book is the pick of the litter but it's in no shape for borrowing or photocopying. I page through it slowly, carefully.

I'm three quarters of the way into it and there's still no mention of Jack Donahue or any of the others. I check the publication date: 1988. Surely there has to be something...

And there is. On one of the last pages.

The picture was taken at the funeral of Sean McManus, a man much beloved in the criminal fraternity. His coffin surrounded by wreaths and arrangements and, off to the side, looking very solemn, stands Jack Donahue, round-faced and heavyset, and over there, at extreme left, caught in the midst of turning...could it be...? The profile is familiar but identification next to impossible. It *might* be Eugene or my father. No one in the picture identified except Donahue and the guest of honour. There's no date, though something tells me it was taken in the late Sixties or early 1970s. I stare at the photo a long time. It's fruitless. It could be one of them or neither.

I scratch out a couple dozen pages of notes. Names and background and period detail. Good, old-fashioned research, the kind of mental grunt work I haven't done since university days.

I check my watch and realize it's nearly time to meet Neil. Step outside to use my cell. When I tell him I'll be late, I want to grab a bite before I leave for Gananoque, he responds gruffly and rings off. Hopefully the news from the doctor wasn't bad. I've grown fond of Neil, despite his quirks and oddities. He's a character, to be sure, but also incredibly tough, relentless once he's on the scent.

In other words, a man after my own heart.

"I've got a copy of the Poldark book around here somewhere," Neil says. "You're welcome to borrow it." He clears his throat self-importantly. "Actually, I was one of his sources. He even thanks me in the introduction."

"Is there much on Donahue?"

He shakes his head. "You have to understand, you can't just out and out accuse someone of being a mobster. Not while they're still on this side of heaven. These guys are smart, they like to come across as local businessmen, right? Pillars of the community, paying their taxes, good Shriners and Kinsmen. Men like Jack keep their noses squeaky clean. Avoid attention like the bubonic plague. And they make it downright unhealthy for anyone trying to expose them."

"I believe you. And speaking of health, how's yours? What did the doctor say?"

He grimaces. "The doctors. The doctors say this, the doctors say that. And when they don't know, they order more bloody tests." He throws up his hands. "*This* is what they say."

"Well, you seem pretty chipper today."

"That's because you got me fired up, kid. I'm in my element. This is bringing back all sorts of memories and war stories. The good ol' days."

"My pleasure, Neil."

"Hey…" Glancing over at me. "You ever get inside 26?" I nod and he brings his fist to his mouth, gnawing it in mock frustration. "I always wanted to but…never got my shot."

"They had Christmas parties there."

"*Really?*"

"Sometimes we skipped them but a few times I went."

"Good Lord. Who was Santa Claus? Don't tell me it was—"

"Just some guy they hired. His beard got more stained and tattered every year."

"And Jack would be there?"

"Sure, all of them. Jack, my father, Eugene, Denny Flaherty…I didn't know most of their names or what they did. I probably got introduced to Ted Hoffman at some point, although if that's the case, I honestly don't remember him. I was a kid, seven, eight years old. I just wanted my present."

"So you had no idea what went on there?"

"Vague tremors. There were pictures, people said they were politicians and big shots but I didn't recognize them. It's not like anybody was going, y'know, *oooo, there goes Jack Donahue, Kingston's resident kingpin.*"

"Not only Kingston," he reminds me, "we're talking about a mighty big chunk of territory. Deeded to him by the Consortium in Montreal, his for as long as he could keep it." He pats my arm. "Listen, kid, you want to know about Jack Donahue, forget about the books and research, get it from the horse's mouth. Don't rely on secondhand information, talk to someone who was actually there." He's grinning at me, waiting.

"And you happen to know just the person."

"Of course. But here's the deal: no recording, no notes, at least, not in front of her. She's touchy about that."

"So who is it? Who's this mystery witness of yours?"

"Someone who knew *everybody*," he replies cryptically. "A certain lady who'll appreciate a night on the town, especially if we're paying. I took the liberty of making a reservation at a little Korean place she likes."

"Neil," I plead, "my budget has its limits. Tell me she's going to be worth it."

"Don't worry, I know this gal. Maggie has a million stories and not an ounce of shame."

I grunt, only half-convinced. "If you say so."

"I knew you'd approve."


The Korean place is called *Si's*. Just *Si's*.

Catchy.

Margaret Duchesne (*née* Farrell) is an attractive older lady—I won't call her elderly because she makes such herculean efforts to avoid that designation. Her clothes are designed for someone at least two decades younger and her hair contains more dye than a hippy's t-shirt. When she shakes my hand, her wrists tinkle and clack with various bracelets and charms...yes, indeed, the lady certainly has a lot of charm. She turns on her high beam smile at every opportunity, flirting with us, the waiter, anyone in the vicinity, her laughter throaty and loud. This is a woman who refuses to let anything vex her or spoil the fun. Ten minutes after we meet she's on her second boilermaker and entertaining us with some fairly bawdy episodes from her past.

"There was drinkin' and all the craziness that went with it. The regular crowd at *Sweeney's* was hard enough to handle but then there were the nights when the boys came in: Dennis Flaherty and Miles Coughlin and that bunch, sometimes even the man himself." She winks at me. "No crime havin' a few drinks with friends as long as everyone minds their manners. Everyone was welcome, cops, villains, the reincarnation of Jesus Christ for all we cared. As long as He paid for a round and didn't get too tight." Surreptitiously crossing herself against the blasphemy.

"You knew all of them, didn't you, Maggie?" Neil prompts her. He's nursing a glass of house red, watching enviously as she signals for another refill.

"*Sweeney's* was where you went if you were lookin' for a bit o' fun or maybe a spot of trouble, dependin' on your mood. Everyone knew it was where the lads hung out and to watch yourself when they slipped in to wet their tongues. You could always tell when some of them were about. You could feel it in the air."

"So you were acquainted with both Terry and Eugene," I manage to sneak in. Feeling like the forgotten man.

"Acquainted? Oh, sure. Terry was married and not around as much, so mostly it was Gene. A rum man, if I remember, not whiskey or beer, like the rest of them."

I'm feeling at a loss. "Did you…like them?" Odd question but she isn't fazed.

"They were never rude, always civil. No trouble at all. I think Gene was a gambler. He sometimes had trouble paying the tab. That's my recollection. Always playin' some hot tip. There was lots of gambling goin' on back then. Bookies had a field day and your uncle was *acquainted* with most of 'em."

"Yeah, that's right." Neil smiles at the memory. "You used to have 'Derby Days'. Plenty of money used to change hands, some of it mine."

"There were guys working the phone constantly, checking the line on a football or hockey game or the GGs running at Woodbine. The horses by day, the dogs at night. That would be your man Gene."

"You say you knew my uncle best. Could you describe him, the impression he left?"

She thinks about it. "Well, I'd say he was always polite, cordial. Neat, well-dressed, no gutter mouth. Ted and him buddied about quite a bit."

"Ted Hoffman?" That gets my attention. "They were close?"

"Oh, sure. You'd see them together, sittin' away from the others, talkin' about books and such. Deep stuff, at least around here. Sometimes if they got too tight they'd get a room at the Marlborough down the street."

"But you didn't see my father as often."

"As I said, Terry wasn't what you would call a regular. Maybe his wife kept him on a shorter leash."

You got that part right, I thought. "But there's no question that…how do I put this? He and my uncle were definitely with those men you mentioned before, part of that same crowd?"

She reached for her glass. "No doubt about it, they were Jack Donahue's boys. Dunno what they did for him, not my affair. I just ran the place. Whatever my customers got up to in their own time, that was their business. As long as they didn't bring it in with them."

The appetizers arrive and she digs in with gusto. Clearly a woman determined to enjoy life. Salting everything but her cutlery. Meanwhile, she and Neil stroll down memory lane together, chortling over various pranks and brawls and misdemeanors, all of it vividly recounted, sometimes employing ripe language and graphic detail. I can see people at other tables are eavesdropping, enjoying their repartee.

Shameless, indeed.

As she's signaling for another drink, she suddenly peers over at me. "I just recalled something, not sure what you'll make of it. Your uncle Gene must have done something out of line because one day Dennis Flaherty had a word or two with him. More than that actually."

"What do you mean?"

"He struck him. Open-handed. A slap, like."

"In *Sweeney's?*"

"In *Sweeney's*. At the far end of the bar. Flaherty came in, saw your uncle and barged right over to him. Gene must have thought his number was up."

"Do you remember when this was?" Cursing Neil for making me leave my notebook in the car. Part of the deal.

"Can't say for certain. I believe it was just before I quit." Winking at me. "Got a better offer elsewhere."

"Meaning she married some rich bozo with more dollars than sense. Gold-digger. This woman goes through husbands like Zsa Zsa Gabor."

"Watch yourself, you old coot," wagging a finger at Neil. "There's a few stories I could tell about *you* too. Like the time in the coatroom with that bohunk waitress—"

I butt in. "What year did you quit?"

She has to think about it. "Let's see, I married Smilin' Hank in September, 1972, so it must've been before that…"

"And you have no idea what provoked this incident?"

"Not a clue. He went over, had some hard words with Gene, then it happened. Quick, like."

"And then what?"

"Then nothin'. Flaherty made his point and that was that. Wasn't the first time he'd delivered a reprimand in public. The rest of us went about our business as if nothin' happened. Because that's what you did."

"That's the way you perceived it? Business, not—not personal?"

Maggie practically pats the top of my head. "Wouldn't be personal, not with Denny. If it was personal, Gene wouldn't have gotten off with just a love tap."

"Right," I mutter, "of course."

"He wasn't a fella you wanted to get on the wrong side of. Some of the lads you could josh with, no worry.

When Denny showed up, people tended to keep to themselves. He had that way about him."

"But nobody ever used the word *mob* or made any reference to what these guys were up to?"

Another pitying look. "Tush, boy. Where did you learn such words? Nobody said that, nobody even *thought* it."

"Did you know he was Jack Donahue's right hand man?"

"He knew Jack, Jack knew him." Not batting an eye or giving anything away.

"Maggie's being coy," Neil explains.

"Maggie's being *smart*." Her drink arrives, our waitress adding it to the bill. The damage accumulating.

"I'm not trying to get anybody into trouble. My uncle died almost forty years ago." I see that a few boilermakers and a glass of Neil's wine haven't sufficiently loosened her tongue. "This is purely a personal matter. I'm not trying to reopen the investigation or—"

"Listen, sonny," she says, not slurring, still sober as the Pope, "I know what *you* say and what this old fart tells me and that's all well and good. But you're not from around here, see, so you don't know anything about what it's like, then or now. Understand? Your father and uncle, bless their souls, may not have been paragons of virtue but they deserve respect. I don't know what any of 'em got up to and I don't *wanna* know. I believe in lettin' sleepin' dogs lie. Most of that bunch is gone now, that part is true. But where I come from, diggin' up the dead is a sacrilege. And that's all I'm gonna say on it."

Neil looks downcast. "Now, Maggie," he murmurs.

"Don't you 'Maggie' me. You're the one who should know better. You've got no excuse."

"I met Jack Donahue," I offer, "he came to my father's—"

"Then you know. You saw." Reaching for the glass, her demeanor no longer so friendly and brazen, her light visibly dimming. "This ain't a story that needs to be told. There's plenty o' others out there."

"Listen, er, Maggie, I just want to make it clear, scout's honour, this is *personal*. It's not like I'm planning on using any of what you're telling me or, y'know, exploiting it for selfish purposes."

I can see she doesn't believe me. "This ain't one o' your stories," she says. "You just forget everything you heard tonight. I want nothin' more to do with this business."

She insists we call her a cab.

"The lady goes home alone," she declares. Somewhat wobbly on her pins at that point, the booze catching up with her. "Mind what I told you," she cautions me, just prior to climbing into her ride, "some folks 'round here got long memories."

I pay the bill (all that booze, yikes!), collect the Charger and swing by the front of the restaurant for Neil. We still have the drive back to Gananoque ahead of us. Throughout most of the journey he's quiet, aware that the evening hasn't been the roaring success he'd hoped for. At last he speaks up.

"You bring your passport with you? I said we might have to go to the States."

"Er, yeah. What are you—"

"Tomorrow we're heading across the border to Watertown. Upper New York State. Bit more than an hour away." Sitting up straighter in his seat. "There's a guy there you should meet. I've already made contact and I'm pretty sure he's willing to play ball." And then he slaps his leg in frustration. "*Goddamnit!* Who'd have thought after all this time Maggie Farrell would turn out to be such a tease? Shit. No wonder that woman has trouble keeping a husband…"

I can't help it. It's just too funny.

For awhile it gets so bad, I nearly have to pull over.

*It's two a.m. and I'm writing up my notes for the day. Plenty of scribbled asides and supplementary inquiries.*

*Certain people swimming into focus. My uncle Eugene, but also Jack Donahue, Dennis Flaherty and Ted Hoffman. I'm gaining a better understanding of the atmosphere that existed at the time, but the details remain maddeningly vague. The interval has been too long, the lives in question too secretive.*

*How much more is there left to learn...and maybe Maggie's right about those "sleeping dogs". Is there any point continuing, any new evidence left to uncover? Everyone from that era either gone or faded to insignificance. Why should we care what happened to them? Out of the numberless, nameless dead, what distinguishes them, what have they done that they deserve to be remembered?*

# *Crossing the Border*

An overcast day, with a threat of rain. Which means it's even more humid than usual. Like around ninety-five per cent. Liquid air. Hard on a prairie boy like me, used to hot, dry summers. I bring along an extra shirt to change into later on. I've got the sweat glands of a quarter horse.

August in southern Ontario. *Whoopee…*

Stop for Neil and head northeast on the 401, then swing south on #137, which takes us onto the Thousand Island Bridge (mildly hair-raising) and, eventually, to the U.S. border crossing at Alexandria Center. Just a couple of daytrippers, looking to save money buying American.

We trigger no alarms and pass through after only a brief interrogation. The American border Nazi actually civil for a change.

Watertown is only thirty minutes down the road, a well-maintained interstate (#81). Even so, we have to make two stops in that interval so Neil can relieve himself.

"And if I stop drinking, I get dehydrated and my blood sugar goes haywire," he informs me. "Man, I hate getting old."

Truthfully, I'm a bit nervous about this run. Our source is an *ex*-cop and, if Neil is to be believed, as bent as a bar pretzel. Retired, financially secure and his police pension accounts for only part of his well to do status.

"How much is he willing to tell us? Isn't he afraid of incriminating himself?"

"I know John from the old days," Neil says. "He'll spill the beans as long as it's off the record. No names, no attribution, that was always the deal. And, ah, did you happen to bring the, um, required remuneration?"

Another sore point. "I brought it," I snap, "but this really is the limit, Neil. Paying a corrupt cop—"

"I already explained that," he says.

To summarize: retired police detective John Wilmer may be crooked but he doesn't necessarily see it that way. He strictly separates his police work from his extracurricular interests. Nothing he's done, to his mind, has ever endangered a fellow officer or compromised his complicated ethics. If he skimmed a bit of extra money on the side, collected a "sin tax" from criminals (or the criminally stupid), who was going to complain? On the take, available for the right price, but, nonetheless, a skilled law enforcement professional, with an enviable arrest record. Proud and unrepentant.

"Did *you* pay him?"

"Not as often as I would've liked," Neil concedes, "he was too bloody expensive. My editors would've gone nuts. But as a source of last resort, he was my go-to guy. Always had quality stuff. And if he didn't have it, he'd get it for you."

"Why not take him out to dinner or buy him a round of drinks? Why pay him at all? Fuck him…" Boy, I sound bitchy.

"Wilmer *knows* things," he maintains. "He didn't get his service stripes by accident. On the force thirty years, dirty as mud, padding his wallet on the sly and he never got caught, not once. That's another thing to keep in mind. Our man isn't stupid or reckless. And now he's sitting pretty, not a care in the world."

"Yet he's agreed to see us."

"Old guy, divorced, bored, living on his own, death staring him in the eye..."

"You think that's it?"

He shrugs. "And two bills are two bills. Even now."

Watertown is large enough for all the amenities but it's still fairly easy to find your way around. An unusually shaped water tower—I'd be sure to take a picture of it later, add it to my collection.

Wilmer's condo development is part of a new-ish subdivision in the east end. An area of low hills, round-topped and green-clad.

"Very nice," I comment wryly but Neil doesn't miss the dig.

"Nobody said bad people can't succeed," he reminds me.

"How about the Bible?"

"Nope," he shakes his head, "not even there. Believe me, I checked."

There's a fifteen-foot stone fence around the perimeter and a guard stationed at the front entrance. Armed. But a quick call confirms our *bona fides* and before long we're parking in a small lot adjoining the nearest annex. We're swiftly buzzed inside, find the elevator and climb aboard.

"I might as well tell you: I've never liked cops."

"It's a generational thing," he remarks. "You see them as the enemy, whereas I merely view them as flawed human beings. Some are good, some bad. Same as everybody else."

"The Sixties were over by the time I was eight," I remind him. "I'm not counter-cultural, I'm a Gen X Trekkie, *man*." Grinning at each other. A few seconds later, the elevator comes to a halt with an almost undetectable bump.

"Just mind your manners," he advises as the door opens. "I remember our man having excellent radar. Don't underestimate his instincts or his smarts."

It takes awhile for Wilmer to warm up to me. At first, I wonder if this is going to be a wasted trip, which doesn't help the vibes any.

Right away he thinks he's got me pegged. "So you're the writer." Practically sneering it. A real bantam rooster, five-seven or eight, maybe a hundred and sixty pounds. Still trim, bristling with authority. The brush cut and cool, appraising gaze complete the picture: *cop*.

"I've done some writing," I admit, trying not to sound apologetic, "but that's not why I'm here."

"I know you guys." Thrusting a chin in Neil's direction. "Always looking for an angle. Something to slap your byline on. I guess you gotta make your buck, same as everybody else."

I feel myself rising to the bait. "I could spend all day denying what you're saying but that wouldn't make a shitload of difference would it, Mr. Wilmer? You'd still go on thinking what you like."

Now his gaze is downright hostile. "Could be you're right, sunshine. You did some checking on me, I did some checking on you."

"And?"

"You aren't famous, you aren't really *anybody*. Some goofy kids author. Could be this is your way of making a name for yourself. Causing a splash by solving a murder that wasn't. You see what I'm saying?"

I'm pissed but must concede his point. "I understand. And you're right, I'm not rich and famous and probably never will be. I'm here, for my own reasons, to find out what happened, the events leading up to the death of my uncle. Because his suicide, if that's what it was, impacted my entire family. Coming out east isn't about scoring a book deal or drawing attention to myself. I want to know the kind of men my father and uncle were and how they fit in with this hidden world I was hardly aware of. It's all tied together somehow and I want to...try to untangle everything so that it makes sense. Sorry, but that's the best I can do. You can believe it or not."

He's giving off *waves* of intimidation and authority, using all his old tricks, but I refuse to be cowed. Finally, he grunts. "I'm gonna pat you both down. Get real intimate." He scowls. "No notes either. You just listen and remember."

He keeps his word; it gets very intimate indeed. And Neil doesn't get preferential treatment. At least there's that.

After a tetchy beginning, the atmosphere improves, marginally.

He pours coffee and directs us to the dining room table. Cherrywood, likely antique, definitely expensive. He produces no files, not a shred of paper or hard, physical evidence. "I keep it up here." Tapping is forehead. Still sharp, still bent, still dangerous. Like a rusty safety pin. Neil says retired cops sometimes become bagmen for the regular force guys. That fits his profile, all right. But Neil's right, it's best not to offend him. Probably keeps his service revolver stashed under a sofa cushion. "First thing you gotta know," he asserts, "is that your uncle wasn't murdered. Not a chance."

"You seem pretty sure of that."

"He was a person of interest back then. You kept track. I made inquiries, no doubt about it. Left his clothes folded all nice and neat on the dock, including his wallet. Climbed into ol' Ontario and either couldn't swim or swam 'til he got tired. Found him two or three days later. What the fish and birds left. I'm told Jack and the fellas made sure he got a proper send-off. Good Orangemen, all around."

"And his motive?" I challenge. "Depression? Disappointed in love?"

"More like people were disappointed with him, if you savvy. Him and some of those he associated with."

"What do you mean?" I feel like I'm hovering above something; warm, but if I get too close, I'll burst into flame.

"The outfit is like a corporation in a lot of ways. A meritocracy, you might say. Your uncle Eugene…let's just say he'd fallen out of favor with his superiors. Dropped down the pecking order. And as far as that sort of organization goes, down is definitely *not* good. You lose status, which means you lose protection. More vulnerable. And then people start asking questions, wondering if maybe you aren't resentful about what's happened, nursing a grudge. It's a downward spiral from there. Sooner or later, you end up in the woods or some cornfield, waiting for a guy you thought was a friend to pull the trigger. And that's all she wrote."

"Jesus…" But it makes sense. No wonder Flaherty felt safe humiliating Eugene in front of the barflies in *Sweeney's*.

"Any idea what brought about this fall from grace, John?" Neil piped up.

"I told you, it wasn't just him. He was tainted by his pal, Ted. Ted Hoffman. *He* was the ambitious one. A schemer, always looking to impress. And when his schemes worked out, everything was fine. But Jack could be unforgiving of people who let him down. Especially if he thought they were jockeying for the top job."

"This Hoffman guy keeps coming up. He's always been this mystery figure to me, lurking behind the scenes, never really showing himself. Like the Shadow…"

Wilmer grunts. "I don't know about that. Seems to me he ended up more like Jesus Christ on the cross." He stares hard at Neil. "Sure you want to get into this?"

"Like I told you, John, this is off the record. None of it traceable back to you."

Wilmer addresses himself directly to me: "Word was Hoffman was a snitch. Talked himself out of some kind of morals beef in Montreal and into a vice cop's back pocket."

"Is that why they worked on him so hard?" It's the reporter in Neil, wanting the nitty-gritty.

"If it's true, the man betrayed a trust. A point had to be made."

"Do *you* think he was a snitch?" I ask.

"Somebody did." Shrugging. "There were other theories. Around that same time, Dennis Flaherty vanished into thin air. Denny was a man who truly had his master's ear. They went back a ways. Jack was mighty put out over the loss."

"He thought Ted had something to do with Flaherty's disappearance?" The sense of a circle starting to close.

"Word was the two of them were rivals, to say the least."

"I see." And I do. "How about this scenario: Flaherty disappears and Hoffman is blamed, so he gets killed and Eugene—well, he was his friend, so he's automatically suspect. Skip ahead six weeks and Eugene is dead too, and if it's suicide, like you say, it's probably because he's distraught over the killing of Ted or *maybe* because of his own precarious position…" I turn to Neil, unable to hide my excitement. "Does that sound plausible to you?"

"Works for me," he confirms. "You can see how it unfolds when you lay it out like that."

"How about you, Mr. Wilmer? Does that fit with what you know about the, uh, organization?"

"I'd say so, yeah."

"It could be a case of guilt by association. His friend-ship with Ted ends up costing him his life."

"It's a nasty business, sunshine. A racket. Your uncle or cousin or best buddy could be pointing a gun to your head tomorrow. There's no loyalty except to the top dog and you'll even give *him* up if it means saving your own ass." You can tell he enjoys giving lectures. An Alpha male all the way. "It's not like the movies, boys. These are grubby little men who make their living off other people's weaknesses. There's no honour among thieves or any of that crap, savvy? That's just made up Hollywood bullshit." He rises and leaves the room. I hear a door shut.

Neil turns to me. "What do you think?"

"He knows his stuff," I allow, grudgingly, "can't say much for his winning personality though."

"Never mind that, focus on the important things. We need to pump this guy dry." Helping himself to more coffee. "Try to ease up, let him come to you. Man loves to hear himself talk, so let him talk. Who knows what else he might let slip?" The toilet flushes, Neil looks pained. "I'm gonna have to go next," he announces, standing, practically bouncing in anticipation. A door opens, footsteps approach. "Remember what I said," he warns and shuffles off, passing Wilmer on the way out of the room.

The *ex*-cop sits down and he and I look each other over. "I wasn't well-acquainted with your father and uncle but I knew who they were. I noticed the resemblance as soon as you came in. That decided it for me."

"Before I forget…" I open my wallet, count out four fifties on to the table.

He looks at the bills for about two seconds, then scoops them up, tucking them into his shirt pocket. "Glad he remembered but, in all honesty, that was the *old* rate. Ah, what the hell." He laughs. "I dunno if he told you but I was the best fuckin' source he ever had. He knew it too. He always bitched about the price but he never once complained about the product." He taps the pocket. "'Just a taste'. That's what Donahue would tell anyone doing business in his territory. Didn't matter if it was selling dimebags in a sleazy biker bar or bidding on a local construction project. Bringing over a boatload of smokes from the States…anything where there was money to be made. 'Whatever you do, I get to wet my beak'. One of his boys would deliver the message. Dennis Flaherty—there was a tough fucker—or Mickey Sloane. Occasionally he'd do it himself, if he was feeling feisty. Take some of the lads along to make his point. You know about Dennis?"

"I know who you mean but I didn't have much contact with him. My dad kept family and business separate. Now I understand why."

"Flaherty was a thug of the first order. A man to put the fear of God into you. One visit was usually enough."

"I heard he slapped my uncle. In public."

"If it was only a slap, he got off lucky." He turns around. "What is that man doin' in my bathroom?"

"He has health issues."

"Ain't we all."

"Mr. Wilmer, do you mind my asking why you're doing this? Sitting down today and talking to me?"

He appears puzzled. "We aren't hurting anybody, are we? Nobody's poked through this shit in *years*." He shrugs. "I gotta say one thing, though: that Hoffman business was bad, no doubt about it. Jack lost his cool. As cops, we usually preferred dealing with the Micks because they kept things in-house, savvy? None of that crazy, gonzo stuff you see with the Wops or the fuckin' bikers. That's why they stayed in business so long."

"What about today? Who's in charge now?" Neil is finishing up, running water, rattling the door handle, being as obvious as possible.

"It's a little of this, a little of that. You got Wops, Russians, Jamaicans, Asians, a real smorgasbord. All of 'em carving away at the same pie. Vicious as kicked dogs. Those old style mobsters like Jack? Shit, these new boys would eat 'em alive…"

"So what did I tell you," Neil bursts out as soon as we're back in the car. "Talk about the mother lode!" Giving me a sly glance. "Now was that or was that not worth a cool two hundred?" Still worrying that bone.

"It was a good meeting." Pumping him up. "This entire trip has given me a completely new perspective. The relationship between my uncle and Ted Hoffman—if they were as close as we've been hearing, Ted's death would've been absolutely *traumatizing*. And he was right there when it happened. That blows my mind too. But… was it enough to make him take his own life? That's the question…"

Neil's barely listening. "Ol' John. I knew he wouldn't let me down. Uh, I mean *us*." Rapping my shoulder playfully. "I deliberately hid out in the bathroom so you could be alone with him. Got the feeling he'd be open up more without a former snoop hanging about. Did it work?"

"I guess you could say that."

"Ha! I knew it!" And he insists I acknowledge his genius with an awkward high five.

Neil has a vague memory of a decent Indian joint, killer curry, but when we find the right area, the block in question has been re-developed into a mini mall. "*Jee-zus*, talk about paving paradise and putting up a parking lot."

I crane my neck, slowing as we drive past. "Half of it seems to be taken up by some big law firm."

"Fucking shysters," he snarls, "I hate 'em."

"You have a rather dim view of the profession."

He glowers at me. "I spent half my life in court, got to know the ins and outs, how everything operates. The lawyers were the worst. Preening egomaniacs—you could never pry anything worthwhile out of 'em…and what they did tell you was almost invariably bullshit. What's *essential* is being on good terms with the clerks and bailiffs. They run the show. The rest of it's just theatre of the absurd. Nothing important ever gets decided in a courtroom, believe me. It always happens behind closed doors. Deals and plea bargains, all kinds of strange shenanigans. I'm not saying money changes hands but I'm not saying it doesn't either. Richest man in this part of the state is a retired judge. I'll say no more."

After a late lunch at a family owned Greek restaurant on the edge of town, we're back underway. The car reeks of garlic and every time I burp, I taste *tzatziki*.

Thanks to Neil's tricky bladder, there are numerous stops on the return trip. "It's all that coffee," he complains.

"You should pace yourself." I signal, shoulder-checking, looking for a place to pull over.

Neil sighs. "Don't I know it. It's the story of my life…"

Hang out with Neil, make another dent in his files, leave in the late afternoon. Drive to Kingston, park close to the bed and breakfast. I can see Kim Warburton watering some terra cotta pots on the porch. Geraniums? I can never get my flowers straight.

Switch off the car. Too much driving and sitting today, I'm stiff, creaky from inactivity. I could grab some takeout, bring it back here, eat, have a hot bath, climb into bed with my laptop, write a dirty message to my wife, call it an early night.

Or I could go for a run.

Ten minutes later, after a quick stretch, I'm waving to Kim and loping down the block. It takes awhile for the kinks to unravel but after the first half-kilometer, I start finding my stride. Once I hit a certain groove, I feel like I could keep going until I run out of earth. Marathon? Bring it on…

*But* I'm closing in on fifty now and need to be more conscious of the state of my body. Keeping in mind that the guru of running, Jim Fixx, died of a heart attack at fifty-two. Shortly after finishing his morning jog. It's okay to push the limits, as long as you never ignore that little voice, the same covert whisper heard by Roman generals and emperors accepting tribute from adoring crowds two thousand years ago:

*Remember, thou art mortal.*

In bed before ten, asleep minutes later.

Excerpted from an e-mail to my wife:

*I'm getting better at recreating conversations. The majority of these interviews must, by necessity, be conducted "off the record", which means no way of preserving, with precision, exactly what was said. So I do my best with reconstructions, trying to capture the unique and disparate voices of the various witnesses. I'll never be able to nail down everything verbatim, an exact reproduction. But it's an interesting exercise and I'm utilizing some long-dormant muscles of memorization and mimicry.*

*My "style" seems to be changing (or adapting) as well. Flatter, more reportorial. "Just the facts, ma'am." (Tony will be pleased—he thought some of the wording in the last two Primeau novels was too "fruity" and, damnit, he may have been right!)...*

## Six

# *Don't Fear the Reaper*

N eil's up to something, I can tell.

I've been trying to reach him all morning and have to keep leaving messages. I'm getting quite annoyed—he knows my time here is growing short and every hour counts. I take the opportunity and drive out to Cataraqui Cemetery and, with the help of a groundskeeper, locate the family plot.

There's my Aunt Gloria (1933-2010) and, right next to her, Uncle Eugene (1931-1972). When my father died, Phyllis insisted he had no interest in all the fuss and expense of being flown back east and interred there. Saskatoon is where he died, Saskatoon is where he's planted. End of discussion. You can see where I get my pragmatism from.

I spend a fair bit of time at the cemetery, strolling the grounds, examining the individual headstones, especially the older ones. Graveyards have never creeped me out. I view them merely as vaults for old bones, a peaceful garden for grieving relatives to visit. No ghosts here, I can't imagine a less interesting place for spirits to congregate.

*May you be half an hour in heaven before the devil knows you're dead.*

My father was the oldest, Gloria the baby of the family, but that didn't represent the true pecking order. In reality, she was the smartest and toughest of the siblings and don't think her brothers didn't resent her for it. She was well-fixed after her husband's fiery demise and beholden to none. Which made her a force to be reckoned with. Her survival skills kept her upright nearly four score years and during her lifetime she took shit from no one. One fierce Irish lady. Wish I'd gotten to know her better.

Neil calls just before noon, apologizing for being incommunicado. "There's something in the works," he says cryptically. "I set it in motion once you confirmed you were coming out here and now it looks like everything is 'go'. Game on."

"Care to fill me in?"

"Come and get me and I'll tell you all about it."

"If this was a movie, I'd pull up in front of your place just as the coroner is wheeling you out."

I can hear him laughing. "Nah, it won't be anything like that. Although if I don't do something about my general state of health I'm told I could keel over at any moment. Tits up and worms for roommates."

"You're a wreck, Neil. You'd better start looking after yourself."

"Don't I know it," he groans. "And the thing about getting old is nothing improves, it's all downhill from here."

"See you in a half hour."

"Nah, I decided to save you some mileage on your rental. I'm down here at the Kingston bus depot, making notes on the local flora and fauna." Murmuring: "You wouldn't believe the kind of people that hang out here."

"Wow, thanks." I'm touched. Sparing me that drive, scenic though it may be, raises his stock considerably.

"It saves us time. Your appointment is at two."

"Appointment? What appointment? *Neil…*"

"I'll be waiting…"


I go: "No way." I go: "You're kidding." I go: "I don't know about this, Neil." And then, feebly: "You should have checked with me first."

Neil's too busy congratulating himself to pay any heed to my unease. "It was touch and go, I'm telling you. I began laying the groundwork when you told me you were coming. I called some people, talked with an old buddy of mine in Corrections and *voilà*." He crosses his fingers over his stomach, looking intolerably smug. "We fudged things a bit so when you get there remember this is a personal visit, part of some research you're doing on your family history. You're not a journalist and you sure as hell don't know *me*, got it?"

I make a gurgling sound. "But—but—"

He's still not registering my obvious distress. "The only question was would he be willing to see you. No way I could predict that. But I guess he checked you out, decided it wouldn't do any harm, so we're good to go. Two o'clock sharp."

It's coming at me too fast. "Checked me out? What do you mean checked me out?"

Neil shrugs. "I dunno, maybe he *Googled* you. What difference does it make? The main thing is you passed muster and he's agreed to sit down with you. What more do you want?"

"How about some time for—for, y'know, *preparation*," I complain. "I need to put together some questions, try to—"

"You know what to ask," he says, "you've been thinking about this a long time."

"Everything I know about the man is shit scary. Double murder, remember?"

"They were *Banditos* and bad boys in their own right. Besides, he was only following orders. Those guys got stupid, got greedy and got what was coming to them. Strictly business. Everything approved and sanctioned by higher authorities."

"He took them out to a barn and shot them one at a time."

"True," Neil concedes, "he does come with a fierce reputation. But he's also spent the past twelve years inside so you'd think that would have a mellowing effect."

"Good God." Bringing my hands up to my face.

"Paying his debt to society. In 2023, he can apply for parole."

"You're supposed to be bucking up my courage."

He pats my shoulder. "Never fear, he'll be on his best behavior. I'm told he's a model prisoner: the screws sing his praises and the warden lets him shine his shoes." I glare at him. "Besides, he's agreed to see you, hasn't he? Which means he must have something to say. That stands to reason, doesn't it?"

"Like, maybe, 'fuck off'. Or 'quit bothering me, punk, or I'll cut your fuckin' tonsils out'. Stuff like that?"

"He knew your father and uncle well. He was there when Hoffman got whacked."

"Probably an active participant."

"He's like a living piece of history. One of the last of the old time villains."

"I feel like I'm entering the lions' den."

"Then you must have the faith of Daniel," he advises. "And I would suggest a certain amount of tact, as well. This particular lion still has a few of his teeth."


I turn right on King Street, drive past the north gate of the penitentiary. One of the world's oldest, continuously operating prisons, it's located right on Portsmouth Bay, prime real estate if and when they finally shut the old girl down. You can *feel* it stretching out to meet you as you approach. It sounds strange but it's true: the place casts an eerie pall over everything in the vicinity.

I pull off and park on the west side of building. It's a huge facility, built from the same grey limestone used to construct many of those downtown buildings I admire. The high, thick walls enclose nine full acres and it's quite a trek from the parking lot to the imposing front entrance. The gate is solid steel, more befitting the castle of some evil goblin king. A few years ago I toured a territorial prison in Deer Lodge, Montana that was only slightly more oppressive and ball-shriveling. I try imagining what it would be like to be transported here, passing through that portico, between those pillars, knowing you're not coming out again for a long, *long* time. If ever...

I'd been warned to bring along plenty of identification and patience and I need both, in spades. The security is tight, as you'd expect. I state the purpose of my visit, hand over the contents of my pockets — car keys, wristwatch, wallet, all my change — and a female guard wands me with a metal detector. Then it's an ion scanner, looking for the smallest traces of illicit drugs (and not always one hundred per cent effective). I'm asked a number of searching questions about my relationship with prisoner Sloane, Michael F. and stick to my cover story. At last I'm officially signed in...and then have to stand around waiting for someone to come and escort me to the V.C. (Visiting and Correspondence) room. No one seems in any big rush and I get the impression of an underlying hostility and tension among staff members — this is definitely *not* a happy workplace.

I've seen too many prison movies, so I'm expecting to be separated from Mick Sloane by a sheet of unbreakable plexiglass, conversing with him at a safe distance *via* telephone.

Instead, I'm led into a room with about fifteen tables and an assortment of mismatched chairs. The space shows signs of prolonged use, the linoleum stained and scuffed, gaps in the ceiling where parts of tiles are missing. The walls have (I assume) two-way mirrors and there are signs posted listing various no-nos, including prohibitions against inappropriate contact. I see a water fountain and vending machine, smell coffee, disinfectant, cheap perfume and stale sweat. Over in one corner, a section for small children, featuring a durable-looking play structure, with a slide and various other attractions.

Half the tables are occupied; at one, a man sits alone.

Mick Sloane doesn't look deadly or dangerous any more. He's elderly, early-mid seventies, and a hard, fraught life has taken its toll. The menacing mien and undercurrent of impending violence are entirely absent. The man waiting for me could be someone's grandfather, although the gaze he's directing at me is far from benevolent.

It's 2:32 p.m. Visitors must depart by 4:00. I suspect dawdling won't be tolerated.

I detach from my escort, slide into a seat across from him. He's not shackled or restrained in any way. He wears a grey sweatshirt and blue jeans. Clean-shaven, with short, cropped hair, balding on top. The chair scrapes when I move it in closer to the table. His eyes are blue and they stare at me from under thick, bushy brows.

"You look like yer old man," he says.

He doesn't offer his hand and I'm glad. Those hands have killed, obeying orders transmitted by a brain incapable of remorse. Those hands right there. Knobby with age, thin and pale and veined. Which finger pulled the trigger? What sort of mind could rationalize such a terrible command?

After that initial sortie, he settles back, arms crossed, scrutinizing me. Not saying anything, just looking. Mostly what I get from him is curiosity, which comes as a relief. When I was a child, Mick Sloane scared me even more than Dennis Flaherty. That ugly, battered face…and never a smile or kind glance. A reputation for a fearsome temper and a long memory. Who knows what contacts he still retains in the outside world. No need to push things too far.

"Yer people come from the north, same as mine. Ulstermen. Part o' the bunch ol' King Jimmy brought over from Bonnie Scotland to keep the Catlics in their place. You know about that?"

"Some."

"You know your history then?" A twitch instead of a smile. "Think ya got it all figured out?"

"I wouldn't say that." A child squeals a couple of tables away, his inmate father squeezing his chubby knees.

"Ya know that a hunnerd and fifty years ago over a thousand of our brethren perished down by that waterfront? People escapin' the Hunger an' comin' over here an' dyin' like flies of the typhus. They put 'em in what they called 'fever sheds' and left 'em to rot. If they'd done that to niggers or yids, you'd still be hearin' about it."

I wait a respectful interval, then: "Mr. Sloane, the reason I've come here today—"

"Course we can't really talk about nothin' important. That wouldn't be, uh, discreet now, would it?" Glancing down at a round metal disk the size of a small plate set directly into the surface of the table. "If ya get my meaning." Rapping the tabletop with his knuckles for emphasis. "Don't suppose we have much to say to each other anyways. I don't know you and don't owe you nothin'. Still can't figure out why you're here."

"My father called Eugene a failed saint," I blurt out, forgetting my list of pre-arranged questions. "I get the feeling he thought his brother didn't get a fair shake from life. And, as we both know, it ended tragically for him." He lays his hand flat on the table, palm down. "I don't know much about their lives or the kind of people they were back then, Eugene especially. It wasn't allowed to talk about him or bring him up in conversation."

"And yet here y'are," he interjects.

"But that's only because—"

He doesn't let me finish: "You and yer family, you're free and clear, right? So why stir things up? Aye? What good will that do?"

"I'm trying to find out—"

"You'll find *nothin'* here, lad. Take a good look around. You're in a waitin' room in Hell. Go through the wrong door, who knows where you'll end up."

In my neck of the woods, we call that a threat. At that moment, I want to throttle Neil for talking me into this. "Well, I'm certainly not trying to upset the apple cart..."

He scowls. "Listen, sonny, the last thing anybody needs is you with a head full o' questions and yer brains up yer arse." Another outburst from the kid, gleefully oblivious of its surroundings.

"Does it matter any more?" I wonder and see his face stiffen. "I—I mean," I forge on, "the events we're talking about took place *decades* ago. What difference does it make, who's left that really cares?" It's the best appeal I can make and he's unmoved.

"We come from a clannish lot. Settle things among ourselves and don't cry about it afterward." His fingers tapping again, driving home his points. "This ain't nothin' to do with you. It was settled and it stays settled, understand?" My display of apparent ignorance doesn't mollify him. "You keep goin', keep doin' what you're doin'…" He stops himself before the implied threat becomes something more. "Well, a person don't know, do they? You talk to Phyllis before you went ahead and done this?" I gape at him, completely taken aback. "So," comprehension dawning, "you're out here, scrapin' through the muck and you didn't even have the guts…" Giving me a sour smile. "You're some piece o' work, sonny. Yer uncles, at least, had a pair o' balls hangin' on 'em."

I hear my voice but can't trace its source. "You mentioned my mother. What does she have to do with it?"

But he's glancing up at the clock. "This is a waste o' me time. You best be on yer way. Back to whatever kind of life you got out there. Count yourself lucky you ain't in my shoes."

And he's serious, preparing to push away from the table, signal the guard and return to his cellblock. His *cage*. And I could let him walk away, crawl back into his hole, but a stubborn streak inside me insists that I not be cowed, act like a forty-eight year old man, for God's sake. So I say: "Mr. Sloane, I understand your reluctance to go into this. That's your right and I respect that. But you seem to think I've got some kind of ulterior motive for being here and that's not true. I'm not trying to lay blame or re-open investigations. My aim isn't to get anyone in trouble. I know in my heart I'll never fully understand the circumstances that led to my uncle's death. But I feel like I need some kind of… uh…" He waits. "*Context.* I think that's the right word. You knew them—"

"Knew all of 'em," he corrects me. "Terry, Gene, Phyllis, Gloria. Knew 'em well enough to know they wouldn't approve of what you're doin'." I don't bite, wait him out. "You bein' here goes against the spirit of what was agreed. You mind what I'm sayin' now."

"I'm afraid I'm not following you."

He examines my face carefully. "No? Mebbe not. But it don't matter." Leaning in. "So you write, like? Books and such?"

"Fiction…just kids' books, mainly, nothing serious or—"

"I read plenty in here. I like that Elmore Leonard fella. All the twists and turns, eh? You never know what's gonna pop up next."

"Yes, I agree, he's very good. Terrific, in fact. Although, like I said, personally, my work leans more toward the young adult stuff…no mysteries or whodunits."

The family is saying good-bye, the guard posted by the door suddenly alert.

"That's good. Stick with what you know." Then he stands, surprising me by offering his hand. I automatically take it. Strong grip. "Make sure you tell Phyllis you seen me. She cut quite the figure in the old days. Turned a few heads. Coulda had her pick. Mind to tell her I said that." An upward twitch of his lips, something resembling a smile. "Stay outta trouble now, hear?"

Subjected to the third degree on the way out. A guy named Bryce hauls me into a cubicle-sized office and wants to know if inmate Sloane threatened me in any way or attempted to "coerce my cooperation". Did he try to pass me any notes or "seek to communicate privately with any outside party"? Talking in a clipped monotone, like he's reading off a card. I'm tempted to tell him to check his bloody microphone but why rock the boat? So I merely say "no", hand over my *Visitor* badge and wait for someone to walk me out.

Beyond the stone walls, the sun is shining, it's a beautiful, late summer day. All the colours in evidence seem extra bright and vibrant. I hear birds, traffic noise, the fidelity otherworldly.

*A waiting room in Hell.*

More like a living purgatory.

I want desperately to be away from there.

Walk quickly toward the car...


As soon as I pick him up Neil starts grilling me, dying to know about my afternoon with Mick Sloane. Making me recreate the encounter with as much accuracy and detail as I can muster. Which will probably come in handy when I finally sit down with a cup of coffee or green tea later on and write everything out (hopefully capturing the dramatic highs and lows).

Neil's disappointed when I tell him that some of Sloane's mystique has been diminished by age. "I heard he had a bout with cancer," he muses, "maybe it's come back." I allow that possibility; his skin tone seemed grayish and he'd shed a good deal of weight from his big frame. Neil can't help himself, picking away at Sloane's comments, trying to tie them back into 'our story'. "There's so many little threads and links. I hate to say this but your mother might be your best bet. Clearly, and I mean no offense, she knows a lot more than she's letting on."

An hour later, talk about coincidence, synchronicity, whatever, I'm parked behind a *Tim Horton's*, Neil inside using the bathroom, when I get a text message from my sister, Connie:

*Heads up, bruz. Mother knows where you are.*

But…how? Crystal ball? Sheep intestines? There isn't any time to ponder the ramifications, my cell announcing an incoming call with the cash register sound effects preceding Pink Floyd's "Money".

No need to check the number.

"Hey, Mom. What a surprise…"

## Seven

# Have you seen your mother, baby, standing in the shadows?

" —the slightest idea what you're doing, do you?" She's already worked herself into a state, so I just sit there and listen until she winds down. Meanwhile, I'm watching a family of five climb aboard a minivan, all of them overweight, big daddy toting a couple of boxes of *Timbits*, everyone else sporting extra-large drinks. The vehicle sags as they settle into their seats. "This is a stupid, pointless gesture and I can't believe you'd put the rest of us through the wringer just because you're having an attack of conscience. Is that what this is? Some way of getting back at me because you can't pillory your father?" Then she gets nasty: "Or maybe you've run out of story ideas, huh? Your Indian series done, nothing else left, so you exploit your family, air our dirty laundry in public." Ouch! "Listen, you little prick," she snaps, her anger boiling over, "if you think I'm going to stand by while you open this can of worms, you've got something else coming. I *told* you," she adds, "what's in the past, stays in the past. And don't forget it." A silence that hangs there, waiting to be filled. "*Well?* Are you going to say something or—"

"I saw Mick Sloane today. He told me to pass along his compliments. Said you were quite the looker in the old days."

She mutters something, but if I expected to rock her back on her heels, I'm disappointed. "Think you're pretty smart, huh? Putting the pieces together, like chapters in some book. Your book," she advises me, "will be rubbish. You'll *never* know what happened, never grasp the way it was, the—the—" For the first time I can remember, my mother runs out of words.

"Listen, mom, just for the record, I'm not even *thinking* about a book right now." She snorts in derision, not buying it for a second. "This is…personal. There's something else you should know: you bear most of the responsibility for my being here. There are too many secrets in this family and coming back to Kingston has really been an eye-opener. The more I find out, the more I realize how much was kept from me."

Mocking laughter. "Yes, that's right, you're the real victim here, aren't you? I keep forgetting what a martyr you are, what a bastion of truth and integrity."

"That's *not* what I meant." Now I'm getting riled, my voice rising, drawing the interest of an old gal exiting the car next to me. "You know damn well it's your fault I was forced to this extreme—after all, you're the primary keeper of the family secrets. Whenever Connie or me try to bring up the past, you either bawl us out or lie through your teeth. You want to portion out blame, that's fine, just make sure you accept your fair share." I switch off on her. Haven't done that in awhile. Forgot how good it feels.

She tries calling back, of course, but I don't bother answering. Neil returns, we grab some takeout kebab, then I drive him home. He loads me down with a huge swack of files and clippings and I follow his directions to a nearby office supply place. Spend close to an hour and forty bucks photocopying material on North America's criminal underbelly, attracting the interest of the clerk assisting me.

"Capitalism is just gangsters in suits," he tells me. "Read *Das Capital*, man, it's all there." Stuck in a dead end McJob and referencing Marx. Solidarity, brother!

I return the originals to Neil and then it's time to say our farewells. As we shake hands I can see he's downcast, assuming his usefulness is at an end.

"I'll stay in touch," I promise. "I'm starting to see the general outlines but there's still lots left to fill in. You aren't rid of me yet, not by a long shot."

He brightens, immediately agreeing to be my "special consultant". When I wave to him from the car, he no longer looks forlorn, saluting jauntily from his minuscule balcony. "We're gonna write a helluva book!" he calls.

I have to grin.

Maybe we will at that.


I check out of the bed and breakfast Friday morning, giving myself plenty of time to get to the airport for my feeder flight to Ottawa. I'm paying Henry Warburton, thanking him for his hospitality, and ask impulsively: "You don't happen to know anything about Jack Donahue, do you? Used to be kind of a big name around here." I realize immediately that my instincts are right but for all the wrong reasons. He actually takes a half step away from me.

"Why would you be wanting to know about *him*?" he rasps. Henry's an ex-auto worker, mid-fifties. Ponytail, chest-length beard, tattooed just about everywhere; picture a beefy Hells Angel. It's like suddenly realizing you've

walked into a minefield and you're somehow going to have
to retrace your steps or risk serious injury.

"Uh, y'know, just part of some research I'm doing.
Thought I'd throw it out there, see if you—"

"Let's go outside." He juts his chin toward the
door. "Don't want Kim listening in." A few moments
later we're standing on his narrow front porch. A huge
bee is nuzzling a nearby flower. Yellow, pointed petals
with a red centre—what are they called? "You want to
know about Jack Donahue? Kim's dad used to run this
place. It was more like a boarding house back then. For
the shipbuilders and guys working at the locomotive
plant. He knew some of those fellas. Donahue's bunch.
A lot of them were Masons for some reason and weren't
too shy about swapping stories around the lodge. What
Artie heard sometimes made his blood run cold. Just
shop talk to them. Shooting the breeze. Jack Donahue
was the head honcho but there were others just as bad, if
not worse. You say you're doing research?" I nod. "Well,
people don't know the half of it. This whole province is
mobbed up, one way or the other. Construction, unions,
politics…they've got their dirty fuckin' fingers in everything and nobody in authority says 'boo'." He clears his
throat, spits. "Should be getting back inside. Thanks for
staying with us. Come back any time." We shake hands,

I hoist my suitcase and file box, load up the Charger and head for the airport.

I spend most of the return flight collating my notes, highlighting important points and formulating future lines of inquiry. There's an enormous amount of information to absorb but I'm a fast reader and have the ability to quickly assimilate and synthesize relevant details.

And yet, I'm forever losing track of my car keys…

The reach and scope of organized crime in my home and native land astonishes me. Henry Warburton is right, they're wired into just about every level of society, their influence corrupting everything it touches. The recent scandals in Quebec, mayors and city councilors in collusion with mobsters. Bribes and payoffs and fixed bidding for lucrative municipal contracts.

There are literally billions of dollars up for grabs and the Bad Guys aren't about to let money like that slip through their hands. As a result, they've grown flush with cash, not only because of their criminal enterprises, but also from numerous fronts and subsidiaries. One article from *Maclean's* provides a breakdown of their activities; it's clear they've managed to insinuate themselves right into our neighborhoods. Mob-friendly contractors pave our streets and build our bridges, mob-owned trucks collect our garbage. They process our meat and haul our goods. All for a little on the side, a "taste". Call it a *gangsta* tax. Like it or not, at one time or another you've put money in their bottomless pockets, subsidizing their less savory activities.

To protect their interests, they buy or rent officials from every level of government, donate to all the major parties, supporting those candidates deemed least likely to rock the boat. The last thing these guys want is some fucking crusader flipping over rocks, exposing what lies beneath. Through fair means or foul, they work their will. Not above stuffing a ballot box or two, planting evidence, arranging a honey pot. Bribery, extortion, blackmail (whatever it takes).

Then there's the "Consortium". Apparently, it really exists, a board or body made up of members of the various mobs in Ontario and Quebec—the Mafia, Hells Angels and whoever else qualifies—that settles disputes and sends regular deputations to New York (where the *real* power resides). Territories are divvied up, deals made, extraordinary efforts devoted to making sure there's no overlap or confusion. Because conflict invariably leads to dead bodies and unwanted attention. Criminal syndicates prefer remaining under the radar, silent, deadly, all but undetectable. A hidden cancer, gnawing away at its host body, causing it to sicken but never allowing it to die.

At one point I notice my seatmate has taken an interest in my reading (a Montreal *Gazette* article on the recent murder of a close associate of the infamous Gennaro crime family). I glance over, catch him red-handed. He's a good sport about it, readily admitting his *faux pas* and offering apologies.

Hossain's from Surrey, (South Vancouver). On the West Coast, it's the Asian gangs that run the show. "My brother Malik manages a restaurant where some of those people hang out. Sometimes they get visitors from Japan. The guys that cut off the tip of their finger—"

"Yakuza."

"Right." He grimaces. "Those guys get V.I.P. treatment. Everything on the house."

"I'll bet."

"It's a private party. They close off the restaurant to regular customers. Malik says there's bodyguards all over the place, very scary dudes."

See? You can't get away from it.

The next thing I know, we're beginning our descent into Saskatoon, the city spreading out below as we start our final approach. I hear a "clunk" as the landing gear deploys (one of my favorite sounds in the world). We glide in over Circle Drive and Idylwyld, touching down around 2:00 p.m. local time.

*Home.*

My wife is waiting, taller than most of the people around her, looking ten years younger than her age. Fit, beautiful and all mine. We catch up on things as the baggage carousel disgorges the contents of the plane's cargo hold, my ancient red *Samsonite* one of the last items to emerge. Typical. Par for the course.

"Oh, and your mother called," acting like she only just remembered.

"She phoned the house? You actually talked to her?"

"She left a message, two of them, to be precise. The first one she's pissed off, the second she's pretty tipsy, slurring her words."

"And?" I grab the case, drag it off the moving track.

"There was some swearing, one or two veiled threats…"

"Sounds like mommy." The file box under one arm, I wheel my suitcase toward the front entrance, pausing while she pays the automated parking ticket.

"I have to say, she seemed…frantic. Convinced you're up to something. Threatening, but sort of pleading at the same time." She takes the file box so I can concentrate on the *Samsonite* and its wonky wheels. "She was especially put out that you hung up on her. Apparently that's a big no-no in her eyes." Pointing out the Corolla in the second row. "She even dropped a few f-bombs."

I shake my head ruefully. "Phyllis has a funny sense of etiquette. And ethics. She's quick to lay blame, yet somehow manages to evade responsibility. Only she can't duck this. I'm not going to let her."

"You've always known she kept things from you and Connie. Both her and your aunt. And they may have genuinely believed they were doing the right thing."

"Phyllis knew all along what was going on. She's not some stupid *hausfrau*, she's fucking implicated right up to her eyebrows and won't admit it. Just because they're women doesn't give her and Gloria a free pass."

"I didn't say that,' she replies, opening the trunk so I can heave the suitcase inside.

"Sorry." Reaching out and touching her arm. "What I *should've* said is that nothing in our house happened without Phyllis knowing about it. Same with Gloria, I imagine. You didn't know her but she was no shrinking violet either. Matter of fact, they're like two sides of the same coin. Maybe that's why they never got along."

"I understand."

"I…shouldn't have gone off on you like that."

"No offense taken. Let's get you home."

The parking lot is a Minoan labyrinth but she negotiates it just fine. I sit beside her, soaking up her presence, enjoying the earthiness and vitality she exudes like a rare tropical flower. Reaching over, I take her hand. She squeezes back. At a red light we lean together for a long, deep kiss. "*Mmm.* I've been waiting for that…"

"I know it was only five days," she says, underway again now that the light's changed, "but it seemed longer, much longer. I can't believe how much I missed you. It's kind of sickening."

I'm touched. My wife isn't an overly sentimental person so the confession is a rare display of vulnerability. "That's okay, shweetheart," doing a dreadful Bogart, "I never met a dame yet that could resist me."

"How about your mother?"

Her jest provokes a shudder. "You have a way of ruining a tender moment."

"Don't worry," she pats my knee, "I'll protect you from the wicked old witch. I always keep a spare bucket of water by the front door. Just in case."

"Sooner or later I'm going to have to face her," I sigh. "'*Come into my parlour, said the spider to the fly'*."

"You don't look anything like Little Miss Muffet."

"The thing is," I muse, "I *know* she could shed some light on those years—if she wanted to, that is." Then: "I wish I had some leverage."

"What do you mean?"

"Something I could use to pry information out of the old girl. I know that sounds cruel," I concede, "but you know what I mean. Under ordinary circumstances, you could waterboard her for a week straight and she wouldn't say shit."

"People with secrets sooner or later want to tell them, don't they?"

'Not my mother. She's definitely the exception to that rule."

"I'm not so sure…"

Back at the house, I listen to the saved messages. She's right, Phyllis sounds uncharacteristically rattled:

*…important for you to know that your stupid, selfish tampering isn't going to accomplish anything. If you think poking around in the past is going to gain you some kind of advantage, you're sadly mistaken. What you're doing you're doing out of spite, trying to get back at me because you can't reach Terry. He's the one you should really be thinking about, he's the one who'll suffer most if you insist*

on pursuing this—this sick vendetta of yours. If nothing else, give some thought to his reputation and good name...

My father? What can I do to *him*? Safely stashed away in Woodlawn Cemetery, out of harm's way. Boy, she's not missing any tricks. Playing the guilt card for all it's worth.

Sorry, Phyllis, but this time you're not going to get your way.

This time it's the truth, the whole truth and nothing but.

So help me, God.

## E i g h t

## *Queen Bitch*

**S**pend the better part of the following morning setting up my writing area, sorting and arranging notes and resources. The project still untitled and, at least for the time being, in limbo, formless and indistinct. I'm even coy with my wife, refusing to describe what I'm doing as a memoir, non-fiction, true crime or, well, *anything*.

I can see she's annoyed and maybe even somewhat hurt (I'm usually much more forthcoming about my works-in-progress) but she's a good sport and I doubt she'll hold a grudge. I've try to sate some of her curiosity by telling her about my encounters with Maggie Duchesne, Wilmer, the crooked cop, and my prison interview with Mick Sloane.

His implied threat has been nagging at her. When I come out for a coffee refill around mid-morning, she's waiting for me in the kitchen. "You're *sure* this isn't somehow going to come back on us? I mean with this Sloane guy. What he said to you, it makes me wonder…"

I can tell what she's thinking, can read it from her body language.

She's worried about something happening to our boys. Our young *men*.

They're getting more and more independent, trying out fledgling wings. Won't be long before the nest is empty. And don't think we don't know it and dread that inevitability. When they're home, this old, World War II-era house shakes and rattles with their music, video games, feet pounding up and down the stairs, shouts and laughter, roughhousing with their pals. Hard to imagine the place without them.

"He's a pensioner, for heaven's sake, you should've seen him. Been in jail twelve years and not keen on scotching his chances of being sent to a more open facility, once Kingston Pen closes for good. From what Neil says, he might even be dying. He hasn't been a factor for a long time."

"But he's a killer, right? You said he murdered people—"

"Ages ago," I remind her. "A couple of renegade bikers. Bad guys. Ancient history, darlin'."

She doesn't look entirely convinced. "Why couldn't you come from an ordinary family?" she wonders. "Church-going people, pharmacists or bakers…"

I put my mug down, go over and slide an arm around her waist. "I don't want you getting all strung out about this. You know me, physically I'm a coward. If I thought there was the slightest danger, I'd bolt like a frightened gazelle." We embrace. Even without heels she's got nearly two inches on me.

"You are not a coward," she chides me, squeezing to make her point. *Oof.* Strong gal. "You say that but you know it's not true." She pulls back. "I'm not sure why you feel you have to do this but I trust you. I want to see you come through this better, happier, no matter what you find out. That's the most important thing. Don't get hurt. Don't allow yourself to become…" She looks away. "You know what I mean."

I do. She doesn't want a return to the bad, old days. When I hid my pain and misery from her, medicating myself to sleep each night. No way do I want to resurrect that asshole.

I haven't heard from my mother since I got home. An ominous sign. She's sulking, waiting to see how long it takes before I reestablish contact. We both know I'll be the one who breaks the impasse.

Finally, after two days and with everything squared away, I call her.

"I hear you missed me."

"It's about time," she snaps. "Tomorrow. Lunch. And come alone, just you. This is a private, family matter." Before I can answer, she hangs up.

Giving me a taste of my own medicine. Not one to forgive and forget, our Phyllis.

"This could get very, very interesting," I tell my wife.

In truth, I'm more than a tad nervous.

Even after all these years, my mother still scares me.


I park in the driveway, behind her black *Infiniti*. It looks sun-baked, dusty and there are tracks where a cat has taken a shortcut across its hood. Probably hasn't moved for weeks. Phyllis, the stylish recluse.

She still lives in the house Connie and I grew up in, though the swimming pool has been drained and covered for years. Not even her grandchildren can convince her to make it usable again. "Too much bother," was her response. She likes my two lads, maybe even loves them, but certainly doesn't dote on them. Modest cash gifts for birthdays and Christmas and they're not obliged or encouraged to drop in and see her (unless they phone ahead first). Phyllis not the warm and cuddly type. Doesn't like animals, babies and most people. A big believer in maintaining her distance, emotional space, even when it comes to family. *Especially* them.

After my father's death, she sold the dealership and segued smoothly into semiretirement. Relied on us to cook our own meals and clean up after ourselves. More like a landlady than a mother. Connie left first and I didn't linger long either, even going to the extent of registering for university down in Regina, rather than remaining in Saskatoon. I'd been awarded some decent scholarships and bursaries, and university fees weren't ridiculously high, like they are today, but I'd be lying if I denied Phyllis paid for most of the shot, including my on-campus residence.

My relationship with my mother is hard to frame or define. She's not a typical parent but, really, is there any such thing? My dad was hardly around—she was the one who made sure the bills were paid, household affairs ran smoothly, our lives purring along with as few hiccups as possible. She doled out allowances and discipline. She also handled bookkeeping for the dealership, keeping a keen eye on every dime spent, ensuring each expenditure, no matter how modest, was justified. Even during slow times and economic downturns, the lot made money. Which was a huge plus when it came time to sell the place.

The woman opening the door to me is still, at seventy-five years of age, striking and impressive. Not dowdy or matronly, the way some elderly women get; she retains her elegance and poise, refusing to be cowed by the depredations of age. She keeps her carriage straight, though I've seen her slump noticeably when she's tired. Hair neat and stylish, clothes impeccably made and matched.

And, as always, mask firmly in place.

"Behold the prodigal son," I say, holding my arms open wide, "waiting to be welcomed back into the bosom of—"

"You're letting in bugs," she says, turning back into the house. I follow her past the living room and kitchen, through a sliding door to the back deck. She leads me over to a patio table, its big umbrella raised and slightly tilted against the midday sun. There's hard-boiled eggs, bread, hummus, yoghurt, fruit salad and some sort of thin soup. A big spread for her—usually she doesn't have much of an appetite—requiring no small amount of effort on her part. Perhaps her way of signaling a truce. You never know.

She wants to hear how her grandsons are doing, pointedly not mentioning my wife. We've been together over twenty years, never a harsh word between us, yet my mother still believes it's a bad match. After their first meeting, Phyllis, the old darling, informed me that the love of my life was probably some kind of "bull dyke". It led to our biggest row, a feud lasting months, its bitter aftertaste lingering even longer. My tall, athletic wife, who loathes girlie things and changes flat tires and browbeats rude waiters. The toughest, kindest woman I've ever met, with a heart the size of Saskatchewan. *Phyllis, you may be my mother, the woman who raised me, but sometimes you're unforgivably dumb.*

I'm about to tuck into the fruit salad when she finally brings up the purpose of our visit. "So, about this so-called book of yours…" I look up, surprised to see her conflicted expression, intimations of anxiety overshadowing her usual *hauteur*.

"It's not a book, mom," I correct her, "right now it's not *anything*. An idea and a bunch of disconnected notes, that's the extent of it."

"You know better than that." Not about to be gulled by her own son. "You've got a bee in your bonnet and your mind set on exposing us to the world." I'm about to object but she fends me off. "You can call it what you like but that's what it amounts to to me. You don't give a damn about this family's reputation or if I'll be able to hold my head up in public."

"Is that what this summit meeting is about? Protecting your precious reputation?"

"Not just mine. Other people too. People who'd almost forgotten what happened. Old water under an abandoned bridge."

"You mean *pier*, don't you? Where Uncle Eugene supposedly made his fateful plunge. I was there, y'know. Very scenic spot..." We're climbing the ladder again, goading each other, probing for tender spots. In a minute she'll be bringing up my father—

"Terry would be ashamed of you right now." *Bingo!* Right on time. "Ashamed and disgusted. Because, unlike you, he knew Gene and loved him with all his heart. And here's something else you should know: no one *ever* called him 'Eugene'. The only person who'd make that kind of mistake is a self-righteous, egotistical shit like you."

"You know what, mom," standing, absolutely taut with rage, "this isn't fun any more, so I'm going to—"

"*Sit down*," she commands. "If you want to find out anything, if you want to know what happened..." She points at the chair. I reseat myself. Wait while she pours more coffee. Her hand shaky. I have no idea where this is going, what she's about to say. She's not a naturally talkative woman, certainly no raconteur. I don't recall ever hearing her tell a joke. She stirs her cup, summoning the right words. Finally, with no idea of where to begin, she looks at me and says: "They were brothers, but they couldn't have been more different…"

*Later, I try to give shape and structure to her reminiscences. Hunched over my desk, scribbling onto a legal pad, filling 8.5 X 11 sheets with a reconstruction of our conversation. I work hard at capturing the essence of her voice, while eliminating repetitions and a lengthy bathroom break. This is not a faithful transcript, merely my version of what she said (and an admittedly one-sided and subjective recapitulation at that). Since she refused to allow me to record her actual words, I'm afraid it's the best I can do*:

They were brothers, but they couldn't have been more different. Terry and Gene: siblings with only a last name in common. Everyone loved Terry, you couldn't help it. He could charm the stars out of the sky. Naturally full of the blarney.

Gene was the quiet one, the watcher. Constantly trailing after his brother, following him like a shadow. I've always loved the word *melancholy* and I think it perfectly suits Gene. There was an inner sadness to him. While Terry gave off light, part of Gene was forever kept hidden, never directly turned toward you, like the far side of the moon.

Coming here from Belfast was supposed to give the family a fresh start. They'd become embroiled in some big to-do, one of those things that quickly get blown out of proportion and then the guns come out. That's Ireland for you.

The final straw was when one of Terry's uncles was found in a gravel pit, practically shot to pieces. Terry always denied it was a sectarian thing but then he'd clam up. Completely tight-lipped. I imagine you could dig into it but I wouldn't bother. What little Terry told me about the man didn't impress me. Just another vicious thug, lured or taken to his death. Probably by his friends. More often than not, that's the way it happens.

There's a big expat community around Ottawa so that was their first stop and then the farm outside Lansdowne. It wasn't like the old country, the religious stuff wasn't as important and there were no prohibitions against mixing. Some of Terry's best friends growing up were "taigs" and he couldn't have cared less. He attracted people like honey.

But wherever he was and whoever he was with, Gene was never far away, always looking out for Terry, an extra set of eyes. If you took one brother on, you took on both, usually at the same time. Farm life bored them and they were constantly going AWOL from their duties. Whipping them had no effect, nothing short of *killing* them could compel them to do chores or bend their backs to hard labour. At some point their wild ways defeated their parents' patience and they began lavishing their hopes on Gloria (who, it turned out, had a wild streak of her own).

They sold the farm, eventually buying a house in Kingston right after the war...and that's when Fate showed its hand. Neither of the boys liked school, frequently skipping, and it was during one such furlough that they crossed paths with some older lads, strangers to the brothers. After an exchange of taunts and some ritualistic name-calling, a brawl broke out. The older boys found Terry and Gene more than a handful and once a truce was declared everyone somehow ended up on good terms. And that's how they first met Jack Donahue.

Even as a teenager, Jack was doing odd jobs and muscle work for the Dwyers. Look on *Google* or whatever, you'll find loads of stuff on *them*. They fancied themselves kingpins and behaved like petty tyrants. Mean and dangerous, but almost comically stupid. "Disorganized crime," one newspaper called them. "La Clover Nostra". As soon as Jack was old enough and wise enough to figure out the score, the Dwyers' days were numbered. The problem was they were *too* stupid, even for mobsters, and the Italians in Montreal didn't like the attention they attracted with their heavy-handed tactics. The kind of stuff that makes headlines. Beating people with ax handles or cutting off someone's feet with a meat cleaver and mailing them to his wife. A pair of sweethearts. One day they were summoned to a meeting in Hull and no one ever saw them again. Jimmy Hoffa wasn't the first guy who disappeared without a trace. But I have to say, with those two it was no great loss.

Their "retirement" meant new leadership and that's when Donahue moved in and took over, even though there were older guys around who could have put up a fuss. But Jack had youth and ruthlessness on his side. And he had a solid machine backing him, including Terry and Gene. That didn't hurt either.

From then on, the Irish outfit in Kingston kept growing, acquiring more and more wealth and power. Donahue ran a tight ship and paid his tithes promptly to the boys in Montreal and New York. Times were relatively tranquil, only the occasional bullet-riddled body bobbing up in the lake spoiling the illusion.

But Terry was growing disenchanted with the life he was leading. In 1960, Connie was born and then you came along. For your father, having children changed everything. He enjoyed being around you kids and resented it when his business kept him away from home or out to all hours. He made a point of having breakfast with us—remember that—even after a late night, sometimes spending the meal in a daze, barely aware of anything we said. Well, at least he tried.

You remember all this. We lived in a nice neighborhood in Kingston, you and Connie attended good schools, sang in a Presbyterian church choir. I loved that our backyard opened on to a park. We had a dog named Ketch, a big, dumb Lab cross that bit someone and eventually had to be put down. Then we got Laddie and Fox...

Sometimes Terry and Gene would sit at our dining room table with a bottle of Glenlivet, plotting and arguing, trying to come up with a way *out*. Making their schemes and then abandoning them, looking for *anything* that might offer an escape from Donahue and his goons.

Except it doesn't work like that. Those kind of outfits don't allow you to retire, there's no golden handshake. Once you're in, you're in *forever*. But they were bound and determined to break free and live on their own terms.

They just needed some kind of angle...

I wait.

Silence.

"You're going to leave it like that?" I can't believe it. "I don't believe it."

"I have a hair appointment." I repeat: *I cannot believe this woman.* "Jeanine will be here at two."

I remonstrate, I cajole, I curse and fulminate, but she won't be budged. "I've said enough for now. We can do this again tomorrow." A small, spiteful smile for my benefit. "It will give you an excuse to come by and visit your dear, sweet mother."

"This is ridiculous!" I'm fuming. "You think you're Scheherazade or something?"

"I'm not going to be hurried," she fires back. "I need to tell this in my own time. I have to get it straight in my mind." Again I suggest recording her and again she refuses. "I have my reasons," she says. "You'll understand some day."

As she walks me through the house, she suddenly reaches out and pinches me, hard, latching on to a flap of skin just above my elbow. "*Ouch!* Jesus Christ, mom—"

"*That's* for starting all this without talking to me first." She opens the door and I edge past her warily, rubbing my bruised arm. "You've made a fucking nuisance of yourself and now I need to do some damage control." I'm cowering in her presence like a guilty teenager, caught in the act. "I've got a lot to think about and I'm hoping and praying, son, that this little escapade of yours doesn't undo all we..."

She takes a breath, releases it. "This could still end very badly," she warns me.

Just prior to shutting the door in my face.

## N i n e

# *Black Holes and Revelations*

I told you, with Phyllis nothing *ever* is as simple as it seems.

She phones at eight the next morning and abruptly cancels our afternoon appointment. When I seek an explanation, she becomes downright brusque.

"There are certain things I have to take care of, that's all. Nothing you need concern yourself with. I'll see you tomorrow. In the meantime, you and your reporter friend should look into the Brockville bank robbery. He'll know what I'm talking about. Come around two. Don't be late." *Click.*

Immediately I'm suspicious. I switch off, turn to my wife. "She bailed on me, came up with some lame excuse. I guess I shouldn't be surprised."

"This has to be hard on her. Opening up to you after all this time. You can't blame her if she needs a break." She notes my skeptical expression. "I know you like to portray her as this cold-blooded matriarch but she's a human being too. Maybe you should cut her some slack."

"I never suspected you were so soft-hearted."

"Piss off. You know I'm right."

I mull over her words but can't shake the feeling that this postponement has nothing to do with my mother's age or delicate disposition and everything to do with her needing to buy time. But for *what*?

I don't need Neil to *Google* "Brockville bank robbery", that's well within my range of technical expertise. But I only read part of the first citation before I'm on the phone, seeking his input.

He whistles. "Your mother steered you toward *that*? Why? I mean, it's so out of the blue—"

"How the hell do *I* know, Neil? She's as inscrutable as a brick and just as hard-headed. Dropping a few hints here and there, leading me around by the nose and leaving it up to me to make the connections."

"And that's your mother, huh?"

"We have kind of a complicated relationship."

"No kidding. Sounds like the Borgias. Anyway, I don't have to run and check for that one because I helped cover it. It was, what, 1970 or '71? Had to be '71. The FLQ thing was '70. The Brockville job was a huge deal at the time because the haul was over ten million bucks and only one guy ever got popped for it, a Frenchie named Drouin."

"Why only him?"

"He refused to roll over. And, trust me, they promised him the moon and stars. They figured there had to be at least five in on the job but Drouin did the full jolt and never said word one."

"Loyalty...or fear?"

"Good question. And we'll never know for sure because he died about five years ago. Fell down his basement stairs, if I recall correctly. Broke his neck, poor bastard."

"There must have been theories about who was behind the robbery."

"Oh, sure. I'd say the one that gained the most credence was that someone put together an all-star team of mugs. Serge Drouin was a safecracker, an ace man. And they must have had some kind of inside involvement because the weekend they emptied the vault that branch was bursting its seams. They got cash, securities, you name it. The cops figured they were inside the bank all weekend. Packed a shitload of equipment in, did the job and nobody heard a thing."

"But Drouin got caught."

"Yes, indeed, but it was mere chance. He may have been one king hell of a thief but he couldn't read a map worth a damn. When they split up, he took the wrong road and ended up getting stuck. A local farmer came along, hauled Drouin out and received a brand spanking new fifty-dollar bill for his trouble. The farmer got suspicious, called the cops and he was in custody less than an hour later. In his trunk, they found just over eight million in swag. Cash, stock certificates, bearer bonds, jewels. The rest, around two million…gone with the wind."

"Well, well. That throws a different light on things, doesn't it? This little family memoir of mine just got a great big shot of adrenaline, wouldn't you say?"

"I guess the obvious question is, how does this robbery connect to our guys? Is she trying to tell you…I mean, is she suggesting…"

He won't say it so I will: "That my father or uncle or both were involved in a major bank heist and got off scot-free?"

Now Neil's excited, envisioning the headlines. "Wouldn't that be something? If we could definitively answer who pulled the Brockville job it would close the book on a major unsolved crime. Talk about a scoop. It's almost as good as finding D.B. Cooper."

"You said two million was never recovered. That's a lot of money even now but I'm guessing in 1971 it constituted a bloody fortune."

"Oh, definitely. The problem with that kind of money, however, is—"

"Laundering it."

"You took the words right out of my mouth. Those bonds and certificates need to be converted and you gotta bet the cops were ready to pounce the moment any of it surfaced. But they never turned up a dime."

"So these guys had to be smart. And, I have to tell you, Neil, my father was many things but a mastermind, let alone a criminal one, he was not." I think about it. "But someone was."

"To hold out so long, those guys must have been tight. Absolute trust."

"Maybe Drouin was the only outsider. A hired gun."

"But a wise guy, he had big time connections with the Italians in Montreal."

"That way, it was less likely he'd roll over on them."

"I think that's sound reasoning. Sure, makes sense. Not a bunch of all-stars, a small, select group, four or five guys, including the inside man. Drouin's a rock, the money doesn't surface and the others end up with a sweet little nest egg. Stashed away until the heat dies down."

"This works for me, Neil, it really does."

"Me too. I got goosebumps, kid. Starting to feel like a real newshound again."

"So we've got Drouin, my father and Gene…who else? Who else was reliable?"

Neil has to think about it. "Most of the guys around at the time were hoods, real meatheads. Mick Sloane, Flaherty, Miles Coughlin…I don't see it. But what about Ted Hoffman? We know he was pals with Gene and one of the sharper knives in the drawer. He'd be in there too, don't you think?"

"Would they tell Jack Donahue or would this fall into the category of moonlighting?"

"They wouldn't dare. The boss gets his piece of the pie, no two ways about it. Anything on his turf was fair game."

"So wouldn't he be calling the shots?"

"Jack?" Neil sounds dubious. "Not exactly a strategic thinker. I can't picture him poring over blueprints and devising escape routes."

"I wonder who came up with the idea? Gene? Ted, maybe? We've been hearing about his ambition and smarts."

"But maybe *too* smart and ambitious for Jack's liking. Could be why he ended up dead."

"Which makes it all the more likely he's our Mr. Big." He grunts, both of us shifting things around in our heads, looking for promising patterns and shapes. "I'm still sort of blown away by all of this. Not sure I'm grasping it yet."

"It's a fantastic new lead. If we can confirm it, we have ourselves a major news story and *you've* got a best-seller." His excitement is infectious. "I'll go through my notes, see if any other names jump out at me. All my police sources from those days are either dead or put out to pasture…but I know a few retirees who might be willing to share their memories over a cup of joe. Old cops are like old reporters," adding, "we don't age with dignity."

"You're too hard on yourself."

"Listen, kid, I'm on about eight different medications and a diet that excludes everything except grains, yoghurt and soy milk. I dribble when I piss and shit like a mouse. Where's the dignity, I ask you?" I'm practically choking with laughter, my eyes tearing up. "You won't think it's so funny in another fifteen or twenty years," he grumbles, "you'll know *exactly* what I mean." A minute or two later, we're about to ring off and: "One other thing." He pauses, clears his throat. "I got what you might call a tremor in my web. Just a tingle, but I thought I should mention it."

"What do you mean?" Although I sort of know what he's going to say.

"I heard from a friend of a friend that someone was making inquiries. Nothing heavy, just beating the bushes, seeing what ran out." I glance around but fortunately no one else is in the room. The phone cord is only six feet long and I stretch it as far as it goes, nearly making it to the sink. "It might not be anything. But I'd say someone's definitely taken notice."

"Is this a problem, Neil? Something we need to be worried about?" Surprised by how calm I sound.

"Hey, kid, relax. Besides, you're way out in the boonies, *I'm* the one right at Ground Zero. If anyone's gonna get it, it'll be me." I'm not reassured and hear him sigh. "Look, we can drop this any time it starts getting too heavy. It's up to you. I'll go back to blissful retirement, you find something safer to write about, and we leave it at that. *Basta.*"

"Tell me we're not in any kind of danger."

"We are not, as far as I can ascertain, in any kind of danger," he recites dutifully.

"Will we get any warning if we are?"

"Probably, yeah. It isn't like the old days. You can't just go around whacking people. That isn't done any more. Well, not as often anyway."

I think about it. "Okay, that's good enough for me. Keep your ear to the ground and watch out for anything, y'know, suspicious or out of the ordinary."

"For my sake too," he reminds me. "You think I wanna end up crammed in some fifty-five gallon oil drum, my ankles hooked behind my ears? Thanks, but I have other plans for my twilight years."

I could kill him but I'm laughing too hard. "Damnit, Neil—"

"Let *me* do the worrying, all right? In the meantime, stay on your mother's good side and that's an order. Who knows what else she's holding back? Right now, that lady is the best eyewitness we've got."


"Haven't you had enough for one day?"

I check my watch and she's right; Christ, where did the hours go? I stretch out my arms and we both wince when the sockets crackle and pop like a bowl of cereal. She comes over, turns the chair around and starts kneading my shoulders, really working them. Incredible hand strength but also incredible knowledge in those hands. Years of training. "Oh, God, that feels good. You always find exactly the right—*ah*, right there, right…oh, *Lord*…" She works on me without mercy until I unravel like a Gordian knot. Finally, her work done, she moves back to the doorway. "Thanks, doll. That's way, *way* better. I started going through some links Neil sent me and that led to other things and…here I am."

"And tomorrow you face your dear mother again. No wonder you're so tense."

"Indeed. But this time I shall be well-prepared."

"Remember what I said, don't be too rough on her. She's been holding this stuff inside most of her life. Keeping secrets is hard on a person." She shakes her head. "The energy it takes not to tell, confide in someone. I'll bet she's suffered for her silence."

I raise a hand. "Yeah, you're right, I have to stop demonizing her. Neil doesn't want me alienating our best source either. Even if I don't trust her as far as I can throw her." I shut down the computer and we make our way toward the stairs. "I have to keep telling myself, *she's only human*…"

"…with all the flaws that implies."

I pat her ass. "Smart, tall and sexy. The complete package."

"Don't change the subject."

Her derriere bobs in front of me as we ascend. "Believe me, right now I've only got one thing on my mind."

"I can feel your eyes," she says, "it's a good job I'm wearing flame retardant panties."

"Guilty as charged," I confess.

"Twenty-three years and I still do it for you, huh?"

"Absolutely."

"Wait 'til you see what comes next, big boy…"

The post-coital glow pops like a floating soap bubble and I come *charging* out of the bathroom, robe flapping open, exposing my damp nether region. "My God," I say, "she *knew*."

She sits up. "What do you mean?"

"This morning, when she called, she said something like 'tell your reporter friend to look into the Brockville job'. Words to that effect." I look over at her but she still doesn't see it. "I never told her about Neil or said anything about a reporter helping me with my research." Fuming while she absorbs this latest piece of information.

"So…how did she…did someone tell her or—"

"Who? And *why*?" I sit on the end of the bed. "What the hell is going on? And, y'know, I was just thinking, 'maybe I'm wrong, maybe she isn't such a bad old coot after all'. Then she turns around and does something like this. That phone call in Kingston...somehow she knew I was there and who I was with. I feel like going over there and—"

"I don't think I'm following you. Someone told her you and Neil were messing around in your family's past? One of the people you interviewed, *they* tipped her off?"

"Must have been, but...who? Her buddy Mick Sloane? Long distance from Kingston Pen? Wilmer? Maggie? I didn't think she knew anybody back there, not any more. So how did she find out..." Feeling blindsided, my frustration boiling over. "What's she up to? Even after all these years, still with the fucking head games—"

"Or maybe she's protecting someone. Like her son maybe." Prodding me with her toe.

"Oh, please."

"She's your *mother*, you big dope. You may be a wayward, disobedient, headstrong child, but you're still *her* child. And that means something. Even to Phyllis."

"You're giving her far too much credit."

"And you're not giving her enough." Mexican standoff. "Are you going to ask her about it?"

"What's the point? She'd only stonewall me or tell me it was none of my business, the crafty, conniving bitch." Clenching my fists, wishing I had something to punch or kick.

"Now you're being mean."

I take a deep breath. "Okay, you're right, she's my mother, she's not out to get me or hatching some devious plot. Leaving that aside, *somehow* she found out I was in Ontario, scratching around with Neil. And now who knows what she's started—" a stupid allusion to Neil's web tremor and I swiftly alter course, "—or—or—what she has in mind. She may *appear* to be cooperating when in reality she's controlling the flow of information, maybe even deliberately muddying the water." She's puzzled by my reasoning but by then I'm up and heading for the door. "I'm gonna text Neil. He needs to know our cover is definitely blown."

"Don't make a big deal out of it," she calls after me. "This isn't Woodward and Bernstein, you know. It probably doesn't amount to anything important."

Which is more or less what Neil tells me when I open his e-mail the following morning.

*Thanks for the head's up but I'm not overly concerned on this end. Bad living and poor genetics have done more to me than any two-bit hood ever could. I'm old enough to know most of our fears are either overblown or unjustified. Our days are numbered from the first faint tick of our heart. In the meantime, we suffer and survive. And, in my case, hope to expire in the arms of a big-bosomed woman. Now if you'll excuse me, I'm going to shut down for the night and take a short, painful piss before hitting the sack. How's that for colour commentary, brother?*

*And on that note: adios.*

## *T e n*

# *Brilliant Disguise*

or as long as I can remember, my mother has
been fastidious when it comes to her appearance, automatically referring to any available
mirror or reflective surface, making sure hair
and makeup met her exacting standards, not
a thread or follicle out of place.

So I'm knocked for a loop when she opens her
door looking, for want of a better word, *haggard*. Her
hair untended, the skin on her face loose and lined. She
doesn't appear to be wearing any makeup. For perhaps the
first time, I'm seeing her as a septuagenarian. It's a jolting
experience.

"Don't say anything. I know I look bad."

"Have you been sick?"

Glaring at me. "No, I haven't been *sick*. Christ, you have no idea how insulting that is, do you? Why do people even bother saying things like 'are you tired' or 'have you been sick'? Don't you realize how asinine you sound?"

"Maybe," I retort. "Or, here's a thought: it *could* be your only fucking son, showing some honest concern for your health. I guess it depends on your point of view."

"Get in, get in," waving me inside. "No need to stand out there, letting the neighbours know what an uncouth brat I raised."

She directs me into the living room and this time she has a surprise for me. There's a box on the coffee table, maybe eighteen inches square, dented and well-traveled. Hand lettering on the side: *Knick-Knacks (Storage)*. I've never seen it before. Phyllis isn't sentimental and over the years has divested herself of much of the past, including some items Connie and I would've killed to nab for ourselves. Keepsakes and mementos we accumulated as a family—packed off to thrift shops or sold in garage sales. Never a word in advance or apology afterward. What's in her house is *hers*, to dispose of as she sees fit. If we don't like it, tough bananas. Her words, more or less.

This mystery carton is a new wrinkle, something I definitely didn't expect. She notes my interest and, to torment me, deliberately drags things out, asking how her grandsons are, even venturing to inquire about my wife for a change. Finally, she acknowledges the elephant in the room. "I guess we'd better get back to what we were talking about. This box is part of that and I'll get to it in a minute. Did you do what I said? Looked up that Brockville thing?" I nod. "So now you know."

"I don't *know* anything," I carp. "I feel like I'm running around like a chicken with its head cut off." Truth be told, I'm still steamed about how reliant I am on her, her special access to events of paramount importance in the narrative I'm developing. "You seem intent on feeding this to me piecemeal, in dribs and drabs."

"It's the only way to do it," she insists, "the only way you'll see the complete picture. It can't be unveiled all at once, it doesn't work like that." Not entirely sure I believe her but we'll let it go for now. "I know you think I'm some sort of moral coward for not telling you sooner, hiding things from you. But I wonder if the situation were reversed, if you would do anything different. Because I think we both agree, the main thing is protecting this family. Keeping it safe. Making sure we don't bring trouble to our door."

"All I'm trying to do is find out the truth."

"Well, your version, maybe." Not giving an inch. "You seem to be the only one with a guilty conscience. And you were much too young to know what was going on…" Closing her eyes. "I shudder to think this might be a crass attempt to drum up interest in your faltering literary career. That would truly be despicable and pathetic, don't you think?"

But this time I refuse the challenge. "Mom, we can keep chasing our tails like this, bite and scratch at each other 'til the cows come home, but it doesn't accomplish anything. Haven't you figured that out by now?"

She sags back in the armchair, the fight gone out of her. "I just don't want you thinking any less of them, your father and Gene. They were good men. Not perfect, God knows, but good enough to know—well, it doesn't matter. Not any more. One thing I'm sure of: things would've turned out differently if Gene hadn't fallen in with Ted Hoffman. He was the one behind everything. He was the rotten apple."

"Tell me about it," I urge.

There were five of them, if you included Jack Donahue, who gave the okay. It was Ted who brought in Serge Drouin, an acquaintance from his Montreal days. The thief came with all the right credentials, vouched for by good, standup people. My father, even though he had his doubts about the caper, wouldn't let Gene go into it without him. All for one and one for all. They had plans and blueprints of the building (courtesy friends of Jack's) *and* they'd carefully cased the bank and immediate area. So it was only a matter of waiting for the right moment.

Reporters and commentators at the time praised the professionalism of the heist. I read a number of accounts of the robbery and, of course, Neil covered it and gave me some inside poop. They punched a hole from the floor above, burned open the safe and took their sweet time removing all the valuables they could lay their hands on. Which, over the course of nearly thirty-six hours (it was a Labour Day long weekend), amounted to the aforementioned ten million smackers.

Imagine the *rush* when those men walked into that vault. Knowing its contents was theirs' for the taking. It must have been like when Aladdin first beheld the treasure trove of the Forty Thieves. They emptied the place out, hoisting their booty through the ceiling and making their escape. Abandoning their equipment (stolen, untraceable). No prints, no physical evidence, except the honey buckets they used for the sake of convenience.

Drouin had the best connections so he took most of the loot with him. Once it had been rinsed a few times, the proceeds—minus handling fees—would be divvied up among them. That had all been agreed upon ahead of time. No one raised a whisper of complaint, including Jack bloody Donahue. They split up, went their separate ways...only maybe Drouin read his map upside down. Who knows? He was the only outsider, the only one who would possibly take the wrong road and find himself stuck a hundred yards from Percy Finlayson's farmyard.

He ended up serving fifteen years, a harsh penalty for a crime featuring no violence or firearms. But he wouldn't snitch on his accomplices, the missing money wasn't recovered and for that they brought the hammer down.

And what of the others? After Donahue took his slice, they were left with a nice chunk of change for their trouble. Not bad at all. But eight million dollars is a lot of money and Donahue, perhaps understandably, felt like he'd missed out on a big payday. He claimed that he'd never approved of Drouin, even though he came with the highest recommendations and performed flawlessly (until his capture).

Ted ended up taking most of the blame—it was his plan, therefore his oversight. Donahue stripped him of most of his duties, demoted him to the lobby. Hanging out with the apes, nothing more than a glorified doorman. And the brothers tumbled down the ladder with him, given the most menial tasks and scut work: washing and gassing up the Boss's cream-coloured Eldorado, vacuuming its spacious interior, emptying the ashtray. Sometimes they collected his dry cleaning or drove his kids to school. Even the lowliest foot soldier wasn't so sorely abused.

It was a hard, bitter pill to swallow but, making matters worse, Jack named Dennis Flaherty as Ted's successor, anointing him the new number two. A deliberate and brutal snub directed toward his former lieutenant. Jack and Dennis went back to the old days and there was a crude logic to the arrangement. Dennis was absolutely loyal to his boss and would ruthlessly carry out his wishes. Everyone would be on their toes, minding their *ps* and *qs*.

This is 1971-72.

The winter of discontent.

At that point, the two brothers were fed up. Ditto Ted. The three of them pooling their miseries into one deep, bubbling reservoir of resentment. Working for the Donahue/Flaherty regime meant squeezing their usual sources of funding with renewed vigour. Everyone had gotten *soft*, that was the sentiment emanating from the top; time to bear down and maximize profits. More muscle was being used than ever before, guys like Mickey Sloane and Tommy Tremaine elevated in status, dispatched on various errands of brutality and intimidation, sniggering as they ambled past their former comrades in the lobby.

But the three "black aces" still dreamed of being reinstated or, at least, escaping the limbo where they'd been consigned. Ted chatted up Donahue on those rare occasions their paths crossed, making suggestions, offering advice. Jack basically brushed him off, letting him know that his opinions were no longer valued or appreciated.

So, on to Plan B, a scheme that would allow them to escape their chief tormentors and strike out on their own.

One thing in their favour was that Donahue's enterprises were badly mismanaged, too little accounting, the organization hemorrhaging money. Flaherty may have had his uses but he wasn't executive timber, fear and intimidation effective only to a certain point. New racketeering and corruption laws made it harder to keep cash flowing. There were frustrating bottlenecks, bags of money literally stacking up. A dangerous situation.

Relief was required and Gene and Ted thought they had the solution. They worked on their plan for months, finding the right dealership, crunching the numbers and preparing their pitch. My father was basically along for the ride at that point; it's clear, it was their show.

They asked to see Donahue and Flaherty promised to pass along their request for an audience, but weeks went by and there was no word, no summons to the inner sanctum. Nothing.

Gene smelled a rat. Convinced Flaherty was shafting them. All of them unhappy, drinking too much, paranoid. Desperate, Gene did the unthinkable. Waited until Flaherty was out on an errand, then hopped the elevator to seven and presented their proposal, in person. Bold as brass. Donahue acted like he was interested and promised to think it over. Gene walked out of there a happy man…until the elevator door opened and Dennis Flaherty himself emerged, none too pleased to see him.

Later that night Flaherty tracked him down to *Sweeney's*, publicly upbraided him and then…the slap Maggie Duchesne (among others) witnessed.

It was excessive, unnecessary, an insult of the lowest order, but what could Gene do except stand there and take it? This was a "made" man, Jack Donahue's right arm. Which meant he had absolute immunity, under penalty of death.

Needless to say, the call from the seventh floor never came.

They got the message.

Be satisfied with what you have, lads.

They weren't. Not by a long shot.

And now they had additional grievances to nurse.

Ted, in particular, took the rebuff badly. Flaherty's attack on Gene infuriated him and nothing could mollify his anger. He had developed a loathing of Dennis Flaherty that bordered on pathological. Gene and my father fretted he was going to snap and do something stupid. They still retained hope they could sell Donahue on their car dealership idea, pull up stakes and start over somewhere else. A locale as far from southern Ontario as they could get.

Saskatoon, Saskatchewan. The "city of bridges".

Every time Flaherty walked through the foyer of 26, Ted Hoffman's eyes were locked on to him. It got to be pretty obvious and people wondered how long it could go on before the inevitable happened.

Instead, they got the unexpected.

May, 1972, Dennis Flaherty disappeared.

Gone without a trace.

At first, everyone thought he'd been pinched. Then, when that didn't seem to be the case, they wondered if he hadn't gone on a bender. Shoved one of his floozies into a car and headed out on a road trip. He had cronies everywhere, from Buffalo to Trois- Rivières. But there were no sightings and gradually people's suspicions took a darker turn. Mickey Sloane stated flat out that Denny had grown tired of getting the evil eye and intended to confront Ted

Hoffman and give *him* a slap (maybe something more if that didn't take).

Others found it highly unlikely that Ted, whatever he thought of Dennis, had acted preemptively and snuffed him. It wasn't Ted's style. Jack Donahue wasn't sure and, summoning him for a *tete-a-tete*, leaned on him, hard. Ted seemed to pass with flying colours but as the days went by and there was no word of Denny, living or dead, the mood around 26 got uglier and uglier. Mick Sloane, interim right hand, started throwing his weight around, putting a bug in his boss's ear about Ted and how much sway he had with some of the others, especially the two brothers, a dangerous situation if allowed to continue...

Jack, of course, had never really warmed to Ted, so he was open to all kinds of slander and innuendo and Mick made sure it got pumped in by the gallon. Ted noticed he was receiving the cold shoulder, even from men he thought liked and respected him. There was definitely blood in the water, the sharks circling.

Then Gene started going off the rails. He'd always been fond of drink but now he was a man with a thirst that couldn't be quenched. He got drunk, he got belligerent and sometimes threw caution to the wind. At *Sweeney's*, staggering, wild-eyed, one arm around Ted's neck, challenging the entire pub to come on, come at them, they intended die together, like the Spartans they were. Even Ted seemed chagrined.

It was foolishness, pure folly.

Wheels were set in motion.

It came to a gruesome conclusion in a park near Kingston. Most of the principals present, except Donahue. Witnesses to a horrible, lingering death…

"—Mick, Miles Coughlin, a couple of other goons to help with the dirty work." Pause. "And they brought your father and Gene along too."

I'm gobsmacked. "*Dad* was there? But—but I heard—"

"You heard wrong." Her voice flat, uninflected. "They didn't give him a choice, he had to be there. His life depended on it."

"Christ, they made him stand there and *watch*? He didn't even like it when one of us got a nose bleed—"

"As bad as it was for Terry, it was a hundred times worse for Gene." She's looking past me, beyond me.

"Because he and Ted were such good friends?"

"No, son." Surprised I still don't get it. "Because they were lovers."

She leans over, opens the box, reaches inside.

And that's when things take a *really* strange turn…

# Eleven

# *In My Secret Life*

I get back around four and discover I have the place to myself. There's a note from my wife saying not to expect her for supper ("Linda having another crisis—long story, explain later") and my sons' daily routines frequently mean extended periods of absence. Jobs, girlfriends, extracurricular activities, the local social scene...my wife and I joke our house is no longer a home, merely a way station.

Part of me is relieved. My head is reeling, still having trouble processing everything. I need time to think, get things straight. Roll up to my desk, grab a handy pad and start making notes on my afternoon with Phyllis.

These latest revelations have completely unseated many of my assumptions; suddenly I'm seeing the narrative from yet *another* skewed angle, the puzzle acquiring new gaps and spaces, exotically shaped pieces required to fill them.

When I finish, I clear off space on a shelf beside the desk, shifting a three-volume edition of the "Shorter" Oxford Dictionary elsewhere to make room for the diaries.

Gene's diaries.

Sixteen of them, to be exact. Dating from his teens to a few weeks before his death by drowning. I pick up one of the notebooks: it's black, bound in stiff boards, blue-lined paper inside. Some of the others sport slightly different sizes and formats — each is at least two hundred pages long.

He was not a dedicated diarist, entries sometimes separated by days, even weeks. I note his handwriting is crabbed, legible, most of the words printed and not in haste. Very few scratched out lines or corrections; clearly, he'd thought about what he wanted to say.

My mother was amused by my reaction as she withdrew the notebooks from the box. "You think you're the only writer in this family?" She warned me about the subject matter. "I didn't read much, just peeked, but... there seemed to be lots of smutty stuff. Youthful infatuations and crushes. Sexual fantasies and all that. He was lonely, horny, needing an outlet for what he was feeling."

"Did *you* know he was gay?"

She pondered the question. "I never got *any* vibe from Gene. I sort of knew with Ted but don't think I acknowledged it at the time. I felt more comfortable around them than the other guys at 26 but that had more to do with how much smarter they were, not like most of that crowd. And, of course, they were careful not to let on. They were friends, they seemed close, but I didn't have much experience with homosexuals so I never suspected anything…unusual."

"What about dad?"

"When I look back on it now, he didn't *want* to know. It wasn't like it is today—that kind of thing wasn't tolerated. If you were a fruit, you weren't a man, you weren't…well, you weren't even really human. There was none of that 'gay lib' stuff. Which meant anything could happen to you and no one would raise a finger to help."

"Including your own brother?" She wouldn't answer. Stone-faced; Angkor Wat, with attitude. "Okay, let's try this one: how did *you* happen to end up keeper of Gene's diaries?" Same reaction. "For Chrissake, mom, we're not talking the freakin' Enigma Code—"

"These aren't all of them. Some were lost, others he destroyed, burned up, terrified his family would read them." Gazing at the uneven stack. "I don't know why he kept these." She glanced at me, giving me her Medusa glare. "You can borrow them but I want them back, all of them. Copy them, do what you like, but I want the originals returned to me."

Sentiment? Surely not.

I promised. Not sure she would have let me walk out of there with them if I hadn't.

Now they're in my possession and I have to determine what role they play in this strange, ever-evolving story.

Which means, of course, I'll have to read them.

*I am a lie. A smiling face, aching from the effort. Sometimes I feel like a creature from another planet. An outsider, drifting on the fringes like the worst kind of devient (sic) pervert. Lord, lift this affliction from thine servant. Remove the stigma, as you would pox from the face of a leper. Cure me of these Evil and unwholesome desires!* (April 13, 1947)

*I can't stop playing with myself. I stay hard for hours at a time. Jerking off only works for awhile, then it comes raging back. Is this normal? Part of my curse? I'm terrified*

*I'm going to pop a boner every time I'm in a public shower. Surrounded by guys, all those strong, young bodies, glistening, shrouded by steam.*

*God, I think I've got to do it <u>again</u>...* (June 2, 1947)

*...asked me why I stopped and I told her something didn't feel right. But she kept fumbling with my pants and what flopped out was anything but impressive. As limp and uninterested as a dead fish. No matter what she did, and she tried just about everything, it hardly stirred. At one point she even started to cry! And now I'm sitting here in a pool of cold sweat wondering how long it will take for it to get around or if like me she's ashamed and willing to keep this our little secret...* (October 13, 1947)

*...each time, looking up with new, hopeful eyes but, in return, only receiving a indifferent stare or scowl. Never that eager flash I'm looking for. A nod, a smile, anything that shows interest. Another long prowl leaving me footsore, half-frozen, not to mention blue-balled and short-tempered. Sick with guilt and desire. The loneliness becoming too much to bear. <u>Sweet Jesus, Lord of saints and sinners alike, either kill me or cure me of this condition</u>...* (March 19, 1948)

My wife arrives home just after nine and I'm still at it. Many of the entries in the early volumes are brief, often only few lines; what Tom Waits would call "emotional weather reports". A litany of lonely nights and unrequited loves, interspersed with lurid, smutty passages of a, shall we say, homoerotic nature.

Her eyes widen as I summarize the day's developments. She sits on the couch beside me, reaches for one of the volumes, then hesitates. "Do you mind?"

I'm surprised by her timidity. "Go ahead. Gene's not in any position to complain."

"But this is private, family stuff…" I wave off her reservations and she has at it. Soon she's as engrossed as I am. Occasionally we read passages aloud, a few of the raunchier bits or a detail about my mother or father, preserved for decades. Sometimes the sentiments are heart-breaking, as when an eighteen year-old Gene opines: "I love Rob and it's wholesome and beautiful, despite my irrepressable (sic) need to feel his cock in my hand".

"God, I feel sorry him. He's overflowing with so much passion but has to keep it hidden, repressed. He's alone, totally alone. I'll bet these diaries were like a lifeline for him, the one place he could cut loose and vent his frustration."

"I agree." I squeeze her knee through nylon leggings. "What an isolated, secretive world he inhabited. Knowing it was mandatory, what was at stake if he ever let anything slip."

"Especially living the kind of life he did," she reminds me. "Ordinary people are bad enough but can you imagine the level of homophobia among the men he hung around with?"

"Hateful, it would have been just hateful."

"Then one day this Ted guy comes along and he finally has someone to—to relate to and for once he doesn't have to keep up appearances, he can be himself."

"But it all comes to a bad end. He actually has to stand there and watch Ted die. That's just too fucking unreal…"

She blanches, closes the notebook she's holding. "I'm not sure I want to read any more. I feel like I'm snooping." Setting it back with the others.

"I know what you mean."

"But it's all right for you, it's part of your research."

"Although I can't deny a certain morbid curiosity, some prurient interest, *hmmm*?"

"You're too busy trying to figure out how this fits into the storyline you're building."

I dip my head in unfeigned obeisance and respect. "Gad, woman, you know me too well."

She pats my hand. "Did you get something for supper?"

"I managed."

She stands, announces that she's going to take a shower and will tell me about Linda's latest woes some other time. She pauses on the way out of the room. "What did Neil say about this latest discovery?"

"Neil—oh, *shit*." Palming my forehead. "I said I'd call him when I got back from seeing Phyllis. He'll be having conniptions." Consult my watch. "Shit, shit, shit. And it's, what, an hour later out east so he's probably in bed by now."

"Try e-mailing or texting him," she suggests, making for the stairs.

I assuage my guilt by sending him an abbreviated account of my day, promising to call tomorrow with the director's cut. I'm signing off when I hear the shower quit.

I move pretty quickly for a guy my age. By the time she gets to the bedroom, I'm already waiting for her.

"Well, well," she says, slowly unhitching her towel and letting it drop to the floor. "What do we have here?"

But it turns out I don't have to call Neil, he calls me. Eight a.m. the next morning.

From Kingston General Hospital.

"Whoa, whoa, slow down," he protests when I start firing questions at him. "I'm okay, knocking on death's door but nobody's answering, at least so far. And this has nothing to do with the stuff I've been doing for you."

"That's a relief. I thought—"

"I know what you thought and I already told you, forget about it, it's not a problem. This is about getting old and being in lousy shape and not paying proper attention to my health. Let this be a lesson to you young pups. Now, listen, because I don't know how many minutes I have left. On my phone card, I mean."

"Go ahead."

"Right, so, the long and short of it is yesterday I got dizzy and fell down. Conked my noggin pretty good, knocked myself cold. This happened in the street in broad daylight so fortunately some good Samaritan called an ambulance and they ended up bringing me here. Which ain't bad as far as hospitals go, but I digress, so let me get back to the main point which is that I got, like, ninety per cent blockage of my arteries and I go under the knife tomorrow. End of story."

"Jesus, Neil…"

"So don't be worrying about *goombahs* when it's ordinary, ol' fatty deposits and plaque that get you in the end. They're gonna have to go in through my groin and insert stents just to keep the blood flowing in my aged veins. And in answer to your *next* question, I'm doing, y'know, okay, all things considered. No pain, so no complaints. Except for the bossy nurses and the fact that not a single one of them is any great shakes to look at."

"Do you have somebody with you, a friend or—"

"I have people checking in on me. Lots of folks have already been by, unable to imagine the world without me."

"It's true, you're one of a kind."

"You're preaching to the converted. Anyway, if anything should happen and I *do* join the choir invisible, someone will let you know."

"I'm sure it'll be—"

"Exactly. Nothing to get your knickers in a knot over." Brushing off my show of concern. "Now, in what-ever time I have left on this fucking card, will you *please* explain what you meant by that last message. Your uncle was *gay?* And Ted Hoffman too? Kid, don't keep me in suspense, not a man in my condition. I've been waiting all bloody night to find out the score..."


"Neil's out of the picture," I inform her. Relaying everything he just got finished telling me, pacing back and forth at the foot of the bed. "I think he's looking at a lengthy convalescence too. He figures he got a concussion when he fell. He seemed…addled at times. Babbling a bit and repeating himself. Not quite there."

"I guess he shouldn't be playing reporter at his age. Poor Neil."

"I feel bad for him. And he's been so helpful. Another set of legs, and he knows so much about this stuff. I constantly feel like I'm playing catch up. Every time I think I'm close to understanding something important, I get the rug yanked out from under me."

"Keep him involved as much as you can," she urges. "You can still pick his brain and get him to check stuff for you. He'll appreciate that. He loves being a part of this project and you've talked about how it's made him feel useful again."

"Yeah, well, we'll see how it goes after his surgery. Give him awhile to feel his oats again."

"Speaking of feeling your oats…" She raises the blanket.

"I started a pot of coffee…" Taking a good, long look. "On the other hand, let's let it steep awhile…"

After breakfast, I go into the living room to gather up Gene's diaries and find them scattered on the coffee table, one volume propped open near a beer mug and empty bag of *Cheetos*.

I waylay my oldest as he's trudging to the bathroom, still fuddled by sleep. It's Saturday so he'll be working a full shift at the gas bar, starting at three. He immediately 'fesses up to the state of affairs in the living room, apologizing profusely. He got in late, needed to unwind and found the diaries.

"I shouldn't have started reading them," he says sheepishly. "I didn't know who he was talking about until he started mentioning 'Phyllis' and 'Terry'. I figured that was grandma and grandpa." I'm peeved at him but his curiosity is understandable—and isn't this stupid project of mine all about the damage secrets and evasions can do?

So when we congregate at the dining room table for one of our raucous brunches, I decide to lay it out for them. The "dirty family linen", as my mother would put it. I warn them in advance not to judge anyone based on behavior a long time ago. Trying to protect Phyllis, but maybe my father and uncle as well. They're not in any position to defend themselves. I know my sons have gay or bisexual friends and acquaintances so that won't be a problem, but a close affiliation with underworld crime figures might give them pause.

Which only goes to show how much I know.

"*Cool.*" My youngest is first to react.

"Yeah, killing is, like, in our blood," his brother adds.

"No, it isn't," my wife corrects him. "That was then, this is now. And, like your dad says, there were circumstances involved and—and sometimes people make poor decisions and choose the wrong paths. But you have a totally different history and upbringing, so there's no similarities whatsoever."

"And the point is, it's up to each one of us to make our *own* history. We're not prisoners of the past. That's what screwed up Ireland so long, people still fighting ancient battles. What your grandfather and his brother did or didn't do…well, in the end they both paid the price for the lives they led. Neither of them lived to be old men or got to achieve anything close to what they wanted. Terry didn't get to see his grandchildren. And, in a way, that's the saddest part of the story. They're gone and because of that they'll never know what they're missing."

A somber interval, then our youngest pipes up again: "What does grandma think about what you're doing?"

Smart kid. "I think grandma would rather certain things stayed buried. So I suppose you could say she's not too thrilled about me writing a book about this stuff. I think she's half-hoping I'll read Gene's journals and decide to spare our family exposure and embarrassment." This sudden insight surprises me but I see my wife nodding. "Even if she's right and I don't pursue the book option, at the very least I want to find out what really happened to my uncle. He deserves that. He shouldn't be swept under the carpet like a pile of dust."

"D'you think you relate to him 'cause he was a writer too?" He looks around. "Well, he was, wasn't he? He wrote in all those books…"

"Yeah, I see what you mean." I think about it. "I never got to know Gene very well. He died when I was ten and it's not like we sat around talking about our favorite authors. He struck me as a loner, not comfortable around other people. Except when he had a few drinks. I can't say I felt any special kinship toward him. Until now." I smile. "I'm afraid from what I've read so far he wasn't much of a author. No Samuel Pepys, that's for sure."

"Who's he?"

"Another guy who used to keep a diary."

"Showing off your superior knowledge again?"

"Oh, definitely."

The boys manage to slip away like noiseless ghosts, leaving my wife and me to contend with the dishes. An old family custom.

"I was wondering when you were going to fill them in," she says, bumping shoulders with me at the sink. "I think you handled it just right."

"We have nothing to be ashamed of."

"That's right. We're decent, law-abiding people. No bodies buried in *our* backyard." We high five. My hand comes away wet and soapy. "Sorry. What's on for today?"

"Research, research, research. I want to create a timeline so I can keep better track of everything. I have a couple more books to pick up at the library *and* I need a new printer cartridge. Plus, I'm going to keep chipping away at the diaries. See how far I get."

"Busy boy. But don't forget to spare a few thoughts for Neil. Maybe say a little prayer for him too. It'll distract you from all that smut you're reading." I put away the last plate while she reaches down and pulls the drain plug.

"*Gay* smut."

"Keep telling yourself you're comfortable with your sexuality." Taking the towel from me so she can dry her hands. Mischief in her eyes.

"I'm *not* homophobic."

"Sure you are. But you try not to be. And that's why I love you."

Well, shucks.

What can I say to that?

## Twelve

## *Mind Games*

I feel myself slipping into full immersion mode, focusing on my research with a single-mindedness that would impress any obsessive-compulsive worth their salt. *Attack* Neil's files, tear my way through them, scan-reading for anything significant, liberally employing a yellow highlighter whenever I find relevant passages. The books I've borrowed turn out to be mostly good and soon they're bristling with *Post-It* notes. These investigations lead to pages and pages of follow-up queries and speculations.

God, I hope Neil makes a speedy recovery from his operation. I know it sounds selfish but I'll be needing all the help I can get.

My wife recognizes the symptoms and, wisely, leaves me to it. She knows my habits, they're as predictable as the seasons. When I'm in this phase, I can't help myself, all I can think about is the project, living and breathing it, frequently sharing my latest discoveries and insights with those around me.

Even if it's during a family meal.

It's nothing, really, an anecdote drawn from my reading—which, in my defense, leads to a spirited discussion with our sons on the nature and origins of organized crime, its hidden but pervasive influence on supposedly civilized, ordered societies.

"But if what they do is illegal, then why aren't they all in jail?" Our youngest and, therefore, the most idealistic among us.

"Because they buy people off," his brother informs him, "simple as that."

"True, at least to some extent. Money buys protection, silence and compliance." I think of the pictures hanging on the walls at 26 Clarence. Captains of industry and political heavyweights rubbing shoulders with a cheap thug. "The mighty dollar tends to have a corrupting effect on everything it touches."

"And if you don't play ball…" Our firstborn rakes the table with an invisible Tommy gun. "K-k-k-k-k-k-k."

"Only very rarely. It's not good for business when civilians get caught in the crossfire." Swiping butter on to a heel of bread. "That might affect the profit margin." My wife has been listening but not contributing much. "What do you think, hon?"

She stares down at her plate. "I think it's pretty indicative of the sick times we live in that these people are allowed to exist right alongside the rest of us. I can't believe we condone it and I'm ashamed to belong to a system that doesn't stand up for law and order." She rises, takes her plate and utensils to the sink. My gal is a pretty black and white person. No confusing shades of grey in her universe.

Not long afterward, I'm in my alcove, going through the file box and notice her lurking in the doorway. "Ye-*es*?" I drawl.

"Isn't this starting to get to you?" Indicating my desk, overflowing with books and photocopied articles devoted to some of Canada's most notorious citizens. "Rummaging around in the family closet is one thing, but what you're doing now, all *this* seems—I don't know, is 'sordid' the right word?" An apologetic half-smile. "I know it's your project and I shouldn't be badmouthing it, but it's kind of expanded beyond the initial concept, hasn't it? Do you even know what it's about any more?"

"I know one thing," I assert. "After all these years Phyllis is finally opening up about the past and that's an accomplishment in and of itself." I lean back in my chair. "I realize my family isn't exactly the Brady Bunch but none of what they did in any way impacts on us. This is like finding out a great-great-grandfather was in the KKK or a long lost uncle served as Hitler's personal bodyguard. Interesting, but that's it."

"But what if you find out your long lost uncle *was* Hitler? What then?" We both laugh. "Okay. I just felt I had to say something. I like how you've been sharing with us, keeping us informed about how things are going. But tonight, I don't know, some of what you were saying...I don't want this stuff *infecting* our family, d'you know what I mean? The ugliness of it."

I nod. "I understand."

"Really?" She smiles, relieved.

"Absolutely. Sometimes I get carried away and I need to be more careful about what I say around the guys. And around you too, I guess."

"Well, don't *completely* cut us off."

"I'll watch myself from now on." Probably a promise easier to make than keep. Because she's right, this thing's really got its hooks into me.

I can't wait to find out what happens next.

Just after seven I get a phone call that makes my day.
"Hey, this is Eli. Neil told me to get you on the horn and
let you know he's doing fine. A-okay. Came through with
flying colors."

"That's great to hear. So there were no compli-
cations or—"

"Well, it took longer than they expected but he hung
in there. Right now they're sounding pretty optimistic. He
likely didn't let on how bad it was."

"He said his arteries were ninety per cent blocked.
That sounds scary."

"Yeah, well," Eli chuckles, "fortunately the man's all
heart. Comes across as a cynical old news hack but underneath that crusty surface he's a big sissy."

"I agree, although he'd probably hate us talking
about him like this. Have you known him long?"

"We go back. I used to run a diner downtown,
some of the newspaper boys hung out there. It was kind
of an unofficial clubhouse. It was cheap and I let them
carry a tab." He promises to keep me informed of any
changes in Neil's condition but doesn't think there's
much cause for concern. "Won't be long before he's
back on his feet. Man hates hospitals. Claims they kill
more than they cure."

"He might be right, what with all those superbugs they talk about. Hey, I shouldn't keep you. Thanks for the update, I really appreciate it."

"He said you were writing a book with him, is that right?"

I smile. "That's right."

"It's about time. The man is living history."

"He is that."


Neil's last texts (composed, in one instance, less than an hour before his scheduled surgery) speculate on what other disclosures Phyllis might have in store in the days ahead.

*You never know. People say things to women they'd never think of telling their best friend. Make sure you don't squeeze too hard. We don't want her going into lockdown mode on us.*

We. Us. I love how he claims partial ownership of the project.

He also thinks we should check out the northern Irish connection, noting:

*...many of the people involved, including Dwyer Bros., hale from Belfast area. County Antrim, County Down. Proddies most of them, I'll wager (although, as we both know, money is a religion unto itself). Well, you Irish are a tribal*

*bunch of bastards & alliances between families & extended kin go back who knows how long. Feuds too: don't forget, the Hatfields & McCoys both come from Scot-Irish roots.*

Good point.

*Part of your story probably has its origins in Ulster. Don't suppose you still know someone back there who could do a little sniffing around on your behalf? Or maybe you could pop over yourself, spend a week or so investigating the family roots...*

Sorry, Neil, I'm afraid financial realities won't allow for such extravagances. Nice idea, though.

*Oh, well,* this final text concludes, *at least cyberspace is still free. I'll see what I can dig up. Not sure how long I'll be on the sidelines with this heart thing but you know I'll be hard at it as soon as I'm able. In the meantime, I'm sure you'll continue to make progress on your own.*

And then one final reminder of the important role my mother has played thus far and how much more she might still contribute as long as we stay on her good side:

*So don't blow it,* he pleads, *the old sweetheart could turn out to be our ace in the hole.*


I've never been very good at taking advice.

Fast forward to the following afternoon. I'm barely settled on her low-backed sofa before I start grilling

Phyllis about Ted Hoffman. Not permitting her to seize
the initiative or control the flow of information, cherryp-
icking those subjects she's most comfortable discussing.

But if I'd harboured hopes of knocking her off stride
or derailing her train of thought, I'm sorely disappointed. "I
can't say I knew Ted well. I'm not sure anyone did, except
Gene of course. He was smart, I mean genuinely intelligent, maybe even brilliant in his way. Well-informed, with
a good, critical mind. You could carry on a conversation
with him that didn't have to do with hockey or horses or
who he was fucking." She glares at me. "How am I doing?"

"Keep going."

"Officially he was employed by the city of Kingston,
same as Terry and Gene. I think they put him in the
water department. Drew a salary, even paid taxes on his
earnings. None of them ever showed up for a day of work,
but never mind. They needed legitimate occupations to
show Revenue Canada." Shrugging. "You've been to 26.
An ordinary looking building, you'd never guess what
was going on inside, would you? But if you wanted to
do business locally, that's where you showed up, hat in
hand. You went in and they helped smooth things out.
Even to the extent of telling you which contractors to
use and how much to bid on a job. But you know all
about that."

"Dad and Gene knew Flaherty but Ted arrived later—"

"Ted was originally sent by the people in Montreal to keep an eye on things. Sort of an advisor or overseer. Jack didn't like it but they didn't give him much choice. Somehow he overcame Jack's suspicions and gradually became his right hand man. Like I told you, he was *smart*. A head for numbers and one of the neatest, most orderly minds I've ever encountered. Probably should have been a scientist or professor. He and Gene would sit around for hours, debating something they read about in the news or in some book. They played chess too. Some of the other guys used to rag them for being eggheads but they didn't care."

"Ever since I was a kid and started hearing whispers about Ted's death, I've been fascinated by him. He's like this mystery figure..." She's staring at me. "What?"

"I'm remembering that time, you must have been about thirteen. You came to me, wanting to know what happened to him. You kept bugging me about it, following me around the kitchen, deliberately getting in my way."

"You slapped me," I remind her.

"I knew someone had told you, made it seem like a funny story. '*Pssst! Hey kid, ya wanna hear something?*'" Her face red, angry. "One of your idiot cousins or second cousins twice removed. There were enough of them.

Shanty Irish trash. Gene and Gloria were the only ones with any decency or common sense."

"That's the first kind word you've ever said about Gloria."

"I knew her over fifty years. Plenty of time to find things to dislike about her. I'm sure it was the same for her."

"To me, you were two peas in a pod."

Surprisingly, she smiles. "That might be truer than you think."

I'm anxious to get back on track. "You were talking about 26 Clarence. D'you remember the Christmas parties?"

"Of course. That was the only time after we were married Terry could drag me anywhere *near* the place. I could only tolerate it so long and as for the people who worked there..." Scowling. "I remember one time, Mick Sloane spotted me under the mistletoe. Trapped my arms and gave me a wet, slobbery kiss. And everyone stood around, *cheering*..."

Usually there would be a couple of guys like Gavin Hewitt or Phil Eakins hanging about the foyer downstairs. Keeping watch, minding the store. There was a house telephone and they had walkie-talkies besides. Everything wired to the seventh floor.

There were other businesses at 26. A law office, chartered accountant, some kind of world famous eye specialist on four. The municipality rented space on five and six; occupancy for the building usually hovered around ninety-five per cent. Security never a concern.

The elevator took you up to seven and as soon as you stepped off, there was Eileen Diehl, receptionist and dragon lady: late-forties, never married, never interested. Officious, pitiless, ferocious; willfully deaf, dumb and blind to everything that went on around her. Made Rose Mary Woods look like Miss Moneypenny.

Off to the side, seated on tall stools to keep them from getting too comfortable, at least two gentlemen of sizable configuration and world-class reflexes. They quickly assessed visitors and, should their errand require entrance to the inner sanctum, one of these sports would hop off his perch and escort their party past Eileen and through a locked door (there was a release switch next to her right foot).

Phyllis would wait with Eileen while her companion, usually Terry, would disappear for a few minutes, collect what he came for or get his marching orders and hurry out again. The first time she passed through that locked door was for a party celebrating the election of a new MLA. Attendance mandatory. A dull affair, even though the guest list boasted a number of notables, including a bishop, the mayor and several politicians and personalities she recognized from the news.

Nothing looked untoward or suspicious. Jack Donahue's private office was conventional and tasteless, wood-lined, with a leather couch and two chairs for visitors. There were family photos and a bowl of mints on his desk. He might have been a Xerox executive or deputy cabinet minister.

Everything that went on inside 26 was very regimented, almost ritualistic: you made an appointment, explained your problem and then Jack would check you out. If something could be arranged, he'd set up a meeting at a favorite restaurant or watering hole and lay it out for you. How the deal would work and, naturally, his percentage. Maybe scribbling a few figures on a napkin but, otherwise, there would be no minutes kept, no record of the confab ever having taken place.

Jack had little to do with the logistics of these deals, the actual nuts and bolts—he barely finished grade school. No, that was relegated to subordinates, usually Ted Hoffman. A reliable man who knew how to crunch numbers as well as crack heads. Times had changed, muscle had to be employed more judiciously. The guys with the swollen knuckles and overhanging brows were mostly kept under wraps, unless necessity demanded cruder tactics.

Ted had an office to himself, an indication of his status within the hierarchy. Gene and my father weren't as fortunate but, really, it was of little consequence. None of them spent much time inside 26, most of their day consumed with making the rounds, doing collections or checking out various job sites, verifying the right crews were being used, nobody going off reservation. Occasionally, a contractor (invariably a new arrival) balked at the system and cried foul to the press or some government authority. He might gain some headlines, one or two jobs for his honesty and altruism, but after a few visits from hostile building inspectors, not to mention a chronic inability to arrange power and sewage hookups for his projects, the maverick sooner or later started toeing the line. Or went broke.

Unlike Eileen Diehl, my mother wasn't deaf and dumb and she was quick to pick up on veiled allusions and dropped hints. She knew what sort of work my father did long before he saw fit to confide in her. And she recognized, far in advance of when he was willing to acknowledge it, that he was ill-suited for his vocation, sick and unhappy right down to his soul.

One source of his unhappiness was that he was, in effect, Gene's underling, Jack Donahue one of those rare people who was able to resist Terry's charm and see the insecurity and weakness beneath. Gene didn't talk as much and possessed a greater capacity for menace and violence. That's what it came down to in Jack's eyes.

He was right: of the two brothers, Gene *was* tougher and smarter.

But it didn't save him in the end.

She pauses. Raises a trembling hand to her forehead.

"I have a feeling this is where you say 'that's enough for today, son, I'll tell you the rest of it another time'."

She sinks further back into the burgundy armchair, unimpressed by my clairvoyance. "You don't know what this is taking out of me. Or maybe you don't care…"

"Oh, brother."

"To hell with your book! I'm telling you this in the strictest confidence. These are family matters and needn't go beyond this room." She subsides, giving me a severe look. "That, of course, is up to you. I wouldn't dream of impinging on your," smirking, the bitch, "artistic integrity."

"Appreciate the endorsement. I know coming from you it's heartfelt."

"Honestly, I don't know what else you want from me. I've opened up to you, I—I gave you the diaries. Tell me what I've done to deserve this treatment."

"Maybe if you'd been this forthcoming all along, it wouldn't have come to this. *Jesus.* You've spent so long *pretending*, ducking and covering, wasting all that energy. When telling the truth would've been so much simpler."

Her face tight with anger. "I suspect I'll pay the price for my sins once the book comes out. Make sure you don't spare any opportunity to tell everyone how rotten I am, how much I lied to you and made you suffer. *Poor* thing."

That's enough for me. "Y'know, mom, the truth is I don't think I could write about you and carry it off. People wouldn't find you a believable or sympathetic character. You're much too cold and aloof for someone with two kids and five grandchildren and—"

"Just go, please," waving me away, covering her eyes so she doesn't have to look at me. "I've had enough of you for one day."

"Believe me, the feeling's mutual."

We leave it at that.

I find my own way out.


*Neil:*

*Thinking of you today, partner, wondering how you're doing.*

*I have a couple more names for you:*

*Eileen Diehl*

*Phil Eakins*

*I think my mother is leading up to something. It's like she's deliberately slowing things down so she doesn't have to face it. Stringing it out. But she's got something to say and I have a feeling it's all coming to a head SOON. Will keep you apprised.*

*Hope you're recovering well, chum. Call or text when you're able.*

*I want you to know I actually prayed for you today. Which should, in no uncertain terms, confirm that you are in dire straits indeed. The long, cold shadow of the Grim Reaper revealing his presence nearby, waiting, scythe unsheathed—*

*Not!*

*Stay frosty, big guy.*

*etc.*

# Thirteen

## *Private Universe*

R eading my late uncle's diaries is unsettling, voyeuristic and, dare I say it, frequently quite boring.

When I said he was no Pepys, I wasn't kidding. Most of the entries are fairly dull and mundane. Gene wrote matter-of-factly, not much for extended, descriptive passages or flowing prose, at least during his teen years:

*Chilly day, snow forecast. Might be coming down with cold or flu.* (November 8, 1948)

*Climbing stairs today, surprised to discover how out of breath I am when I get to the top. A fold of flab on my gut. More exercise, cut out smoking...* (July 9, 1949)

*...Leafs lose again, this time to the Wings, and now I'm down $50 on them in the past two weeks. I thought they were supposed to be better this year! They should get rid of their so-called coach and ship half the team down to the farm club....* (December 21, 1949)

His reflections get longer and more detailed as the years pass (and he matured), but I'm not holding out much hope that his skills as a wordsmith will improve dramatically. I fear it's going to be a chore sifting through hundreds and hundreds of pages in order to find a few nuggets of gold.

So far I've gotten through the first few volumes and, as Phyllis warned, there are some passages that are truly cringeworthy. Reading someone else's sexual fantasies is a hair-raising experience and starting from his mid-late teens, Gene didn't pull any punches. He was up for just about anything as long as it was with a fit, male partner of the same orientation. Age, color or creed optional. Browse this stuff as anonymous porn and it's hilarious; read it in your uncle's handwriting and it's just plain *weird*.

But along with the graphic bits, there are sections when he retreats into self-loathing, quoting from the *Book of Job* and railing about his "sickness". His piety seems forced, desperate, especially when a page later he's writing about needing to be held, cradled in the strong, musky embrace of a man who cares for him.

Then there's this touching entry, written shortly after his nineteenth birthday:

*Andy, I <u>love</u> you and <u>crave</u> you. I know you'll never read this or have any awareness of the way I'm feeling. My thoughts would disgust you, my desires enrage you. We're around each other and there's always physical contact, playfighting and roughhousing. It's gotten the point where we can finish each other's sentences. Those long walks, hours in your company, talking about every-thing except what I wish I could say. Which is <u>I love you, I love you, I love you</u>…*

Followed inevitably by:

*I hate my perversion and hate its source, which is my twisted and godforsaken soul. I don't know what I did to deserve this curse but it must have been a greivous (sic), mortal insult against God. I've been reading about reincarnation, a person being born over and over again, and I wonder if this, maybe, isn't part of the answer. In a previous life I must have been a terrible sinner and now I'm paying the price. My <u>sick desires</u> and <u>unnat-ural thoughts</u>. Things I can share with neither friend or family. I bear the stigmata alone, with no one to bind my leaking wounds…*

I take special note of passages alluding to my father:

*...my brother is one of those people who's* (sic) *mind is uncomplicated and straightforward. It's not that he's stupid, more like Terry's way of looking at things doesn't allow for anything more complex than what's going on inside an engine block. Sometimes when we're talking about something in the news, I realize how naïve he is. He's the older brother, yet I often find myself explaining things, trying to make him see the world and how it really works.* (March 8, 1950)

And then an undated entry, a few pages later:

*Terry told me today I "think too much" and maybe he has a point. His life is so much <u>easier</u> than mine, nothing really seems to affect him. He's always "good time Terry", ready with a joke or a pint, sitting down with you and bending your ear. It's impossible not to like him, even love him. But I also get a sense that he uses his charm and humour to keep people at a distance, so they don't get too close. In my less kind moments, I wonder if his "act" isn't covering up the fact that behind that laughing face there really isn't a whole lot to see.*

A harsh assessment but Gene never intended for anyone else to read it. Strictly for his eyes only.

Many, many pages are taken up by Gene's relent-less pursuit of a sexual partner, walking midnight streets, lurking down the by docks or in dives, looking for action, even if it's rough trade.

There was a harrowing back alley encounter in June, 1950, when a surreptitious grope turned into an assault and, by the sound of it, quite a severe beating:

*…hurt everywhere, reminded of a dog I once saw run down by a car. Dragging itself along the street, half its bones shattered. Bastard worked me over like Rocky Marciano. So friendly and obliging, never saw it coming. Even let me put my hand on him just before butting me with his head. Explosion of pain and then he was using his fists, feet, even the lid off a metal trash can. Took my wallet for good measure.*

*I am a perfect fool, fully deserving of my present condi-tion. "Derek" (the name he used) might have killed me, I think. There was so much rage. Probably due to some aspect he's repressing within himself. But something scared him off and the next thing I knew, a stranger was leaning over me, offering help. Fortunately my pants were still buttoned and my Jolly Roger tucked away. No hint that it was anything more than an ordinary robbery. Thank God…*

You have to feel for the guy. This was two decades prior to Stonewall, the gay lifestyle still very much under-ground, largely unacknowledged or ignored by straight society. Anyone coming out of the closet risked being shunned, disowned or worse. And Gene didn't know anyone or dare approach someone and ask what he should do, where he could meet men of his persuasion. And even if such a place existed, he ran the risk of being *seen*, an acquaintance spotting him exiting a notorious hangout and haven for queers.

His life would be over.

Then one night (August 4, 1950) he was sitting on a bench in City Park, lonely and disconsolate, and out of the near dark someone emerged, taking a seat beside him. An older gentleman, nattily dressed, appearing very prim and proper. I'll let Gene describe what happened next:

*It's been over a minute and neither of us has said anything, not even to exchange a polite "good evening". I'm thinking that he must be able to hear my heart beating. But perhaps he's nervous too, uncertain how to proceed in case I turn out to be another "Derek". I look over at him, but it's so dark, I can't see his eyes or the expression on his face.*

*"Come with me," he says at last. He rises and begins to walk away at a rapid pace, while I trot after him like a faithful puppy. On a street next to the park, his vehicle, a late-model Caddy. Big as a boat. Smelled like new leather and expensive cigars. He turns on the radio to a jazz station out of Montreal. We barely speak during the drive to the edge of the city. Eventually he turns down a service road, pulling to the side.*

*Switching off the engine, he speaks: "I want to touch you. Enjoy you. You're young and I want to feel you…" Gazing at me, the level of his hunger disturbing and exciting too. "You don't have to do anything. Just let me please you." He squeezes my arm. "My God, you're strong. Fit, like a young bull. Right at your peak." Dragging his hands across my chest, then diving for my crotch. I hear him moan but when I reach for him, he swats my hand away. "Not me," he says, tugging open my zipper, peeling down my underwear, grasping me tightly. "Just you…"*

And I think we'll leave it there. Depictions of sex in books and movies always make me squeamish and Gene's writing is pretty lurid. If someone put together an anthology of badly written sex scenes, some of his would definitely make strong contenders. He regularly employs terms like "purple-veined rod", "spurting muck", "muck-swollen sac" and so on. No sense of poetry or eroticism. Made Charles Bukowski seem positively lyrical by comparison.

I suppose my wife is right, I'm probably homophobic to some extent. Not unusual for guys of my generation but that's no excuse. She's far more tolerant and liberal than I am and the one time we worked up the nerve to rent a hardcore porn flick, she claimed to enjoy it, whereas I squirmed uncomfortably right to the end.

Homophobic, repressed, prudish...I'm not coming off very well, am I?

Following that initial encounter, Gene's fortunes changed dramatically. After "Roger" had satisfied himself, he was gracious enough to give Gene the skinny on the local spots where men cruised for action, demonstrating some of the subtle signals and gestures homosexuals use to indicate their availability and preferences. For Gene, it was a regular tutorial.

Right about that time his employment prospects began to look up as well. He'd managed to finish high school, barely, and then right away started doing odd jobs for Jack Donahue, pitching in when he needed extra hands. The Dwyers were on thin ice and plans were afoot to supplant them. Plans that would eventually lead to that ill-fated, one way trip to Hull. Jack was riding high, scheming his big move, telling the brothers it was only a matter of time. When he wasn't with Terry and Donahue, Gene was hustling for a buck, driving a fuel truck or helping a friend in the siding business, getting paid under the table. What energy that was left over went into his nightly pursuits. The encounters often brief and intense, meriting brusque notations:

*...inside a CN lineman's hut, jerking, only 5 inches but thick...*

*...young waiter, possibly Philipino* (sic), *small, tight ass...*

*...backseat action...bad body odour, ugly whiskers, could not get satisfaction...*

There are more and more references to "J" and "J.D."—then, as if realizing the silliness of such subterfuges, "Jack" and "our friend Jack":

*Jack in his cups again, complaining that he needs boys like Terry and me to help "set things straight". He's indiscreet, letting us in on the nuts and bolts of the Dwyers' operation. I warn Terry we're getting too tangled up in Jack's affairs but my brilliant big brother merely says not to worry, Jack has everything well in hand. Terry's the type of guy who'll wander into a train tunnel to find out where the light's coming from...* (March 19, 1952)

Only my wife and I for supper so I can give a fairly unexpurgated account of my afternoon reading (although I wait until we've polished off the main course).

"I know you're having a hard time with some of this, but you also need to cut the guy some slack. Reading a diary is like being granted access to someone else's mind. I wonder what you'd think if you could read some of *my* private thoughts." Not being playful, dead serious. "You might not like me very much. There are things we keep from each other, resentments, little sparks of anger, even hate."

"Okay, granted, but—"

"Those diaries are the only place where Gene is free to express who he is. His deepest, darkest desires. He's really talking to *himself*. You're like an eavesdropper, lurking around a corner, listening in."

I'm stung by the comparison but also recognize its essential accuracy. "Hey, whose uncle is this anyway?" I joke.

"I don't want you judging him too harshly and have that affect the way you approach the book."

"Book?" The very picture of innocence. "Who said anything about a book?"

"I see you making notes. *Lots* of notes. You even started a new black binder. You only do that if it's a serious project."

"Egad, I married Sherlock Holmes."

"Nancy Drew, actually." Looking so smug I want to throttle her. "Sherlock Holmes was a misogynist."

"Getting back to the matter at hand…say this alleged book *did* exist, and I don't mean merely in your over-wrought imagination. How would *you* approach it? What's the key, the *macguffin* that ties everything together?"

"I see it as a love story," she replies, without hesitation. "You're hung up on the secrets and dishonesty, but *love* is at the root of it. Trust me."

"You mean 'the love that dare not speak its name'?" Half in jest.

"Not only that. There's also the love between two brothers. Is there any closer bond than that?"

"*Irish* brothers," I remind her.

"You act like you come from this poisonous family line. But you're not recognizing the strength I see there. Your grandparents, moving to Canada to get their children away from a war zone. That took courage. And your father—your mother talks about how he wanted out of that life. That shows courage. You too…you're an amazingly brave and willful man." She reddens. "Why are you staring at me like that?"

"I'm just…blown away." And it's true, I am. "In another minute I'll be hearing syrupy strings and—"

"Okay, okay," she grins, ducking her head, "but you know what I mean."

"I do and I appreciate it." Raising her hand to my lips, kissing it. "Some people have archbishops and prime ministers dangling from their family trees. I, on the other hand, do not. My dad and uncle were, oh, yeah, *gangsters*. They operated on the wrong side of the law and for their own selfish interests. They may have regretted it but that's the reality. Nobody's blameless here, including Gene. I've been reading his diaries, remember, and so far I'd say he isn't living up to his status of 'failed saint'. I'm not getting a whole lotta love, sweetheart. Lust, yes, love, *no*."

"That's because you haven't gotten to the part with — what's his name — Ted, yet."

"Hope I get there pretty quick, the section I'm reading now is really dragging. Sex, dog races and betting on the Maple Leafs seem to be his major preoccupations."

"But you'll leave it for tonight though."

"Oh?"

"Let's watch a movie instead."

She's not usually pushy like this and I'm thinking to myself, *right, mate, you've been spending wayyyy too much time on your family's checkered past, you need to deal with the here and now.* "As long as it's not a rom-com or one of your kung fu flicks."

"Yay!"

"And nothing with what's his name in it, the one you moon over like some kind of — "

"Right," she says, "like you and that brunette with the bushy eyebrows and huge tits..." We're laughing, making significant eye contact. It'll be a miracle if we get through the opening credits.

And the boys might not be home for hours.

# Fourteen

## *Secret Lovers*

y wife is absolutely correct, my notes are indeed piling up, an accumulation of pages that's already quite daunting. A general outline and sequence of events roughed out, the principal players better defined…and it's becoming clearer and clearer how Gene ended up on that dock, one summer night back in 1972.

But there are still inconsistencies, unknowns. My internal editor says too much of it doesn't pass muster. There's no flow to the story, it progresses by fits and starts. Characters disappear for long periods of time and then crop up again, with no explanation as to what they've been doing in the meantime.

Gene's diaries have been invaluable and I certainly have a fuller, richer view of his personality and some of the others in his circle. But at some point all these pages and resources I've assembled have to start condensing down into a version of events that is narratively sound, while presenting a credible and authentic depiction of what actually happened.

Where does my father fit into it? So far he remains a peripheral figure, making the occasional appearance, earning a few jibes from Gene but never really stepping into the spotlight.

Dad died when I was fifteen years old, so I was only beginning to understand him as a man, rather than a parent and authority figure. He spent extended periods of time at the dealership, selling cars, arranging financing, rallying the salesmen, riding herd over his mechanics who, according to him, were the worst slackers and ne'er do wells he'd ever encountered. "Lazier 'n cut dogs," I remember him employing that description on numerous occasions when referring to his grease monkeys.

From what I remember of my visits to the car lot, he was universally well-liked by his employees, even those lazy, shiftless mechanics grinning and waving when they spotted him making the rounds, his son at his side. Sometimes a pair of stained coveralls would be provided and there I'd be, under a hoist with one of the crew, assisting an oil change or checking the condition of front and rear brakes. Thanks to their tutelage, I'm not completely useless around vehicles—for that, I guess I should be grateful.

I enjoyed my time with my father but those bonding sessions were few and far between. His business was successful, he was active in the community, a member of the Elks and the Lions, vice president of the Saskatoon Chamber of Commerce and so on. He provided us with a good life, a big house, all the amenities, including a back-yard pool to frolic in; the downside was we had to accept that he wasn't going to be around much.

Gene's depiction of my father as well-meaning dope, genial, fun-loving and uncomplicated, corresponds with my grownup impressions of a man dead over thirty years. It is not an overly attractive portrait, but I have to concede it's rendered with affection and brotherly insight. My father was *not* a genius or deep thinker. Sophisticated? He loved muscle cars, peanut butter and banana sandwiches and Canadian rye whiskey. He may have been well off but he still had the tastes and sensibilities of someone from the working class. My mother tells a story about a committee from an art gallery approaching dad, seeking help with a fund-raising campaign. "Folks," he is alleged to have told them, "to me, art is something my kids tape to our fridge. And I don't have to pay a dime for that."

End of meeting.


I discover a gap in the diaries, volumes covering the mid-Fifties missing in action. What was Gene up to? What was he learning, about himself and the world around him? We'll never know.

The next journal records various trips to (ironically, considering his brother's aforementioned philistinism) some of the region's art galleries and museums. He admits in one entry that he's cruising, believing it likelier to find effeminate men in those surroundings. But his interest in the arts seems genuine, even if his education and background put him at a disadvantage. His observations, sometimes written on the spot, rooted before a particular work, are often facile and obvious as he struggles to express himself with his limited vocabulary and superficial knowledge of the artist and subject matter. But he tries and every once in awhile manages one of these:

*...clouds and landscapes seem to be the primary fixations of British painters. Take a Limey artist to Ireland during the Famine and he'd have painted out the corpses because they ruined the beautiful scenery.* (June 1, 1958)

Gene's also a voracious reader, something he boasts about frequently (revealing his insecurities). In his late teens and early twenties it's Kerouac and Hemingway and Steinbeck. As he gets older he switches to Mailer and Irwin Shaw, even taking a stab at Dostoevsky. But he finds to his chagrin that most Irish writers leave him cold, including:

*…Joyce makes me feel like he's laughing at me, even The Dubliners, which is (supposedly!) his easiest book. Flashing his brains and then his arse. My father always said Parnell was a fool, that the Irish forever put their faith in fools because they're reminded of themselves. But I won't let Mr. Joyce make a fool out of me, he can take his monkey business elsewhere…* (March 12, 1959)

Mind you, I don't think he was much of a talent spotter:

*I don't get this Vonnegut guy and after reading his so-called science fiction novel The Sirens of Titan, I doubt very much if we'll be hearing from him ever again. Heinlein could take this phony out to the woodshed and show him a thing or two.* (April 12, 1960)

He complains endlessly that no one in his circle of acquaintances is a reader and how it's pointless pushing books on people who place so little importance on words, at least printed ones, preferring to experience life more directly.

And the pursuit of sex and love (in that order) continues apace. He enters into a six-month affair with the night manager of the Kingston Marriott (Frank Delveccio), but the relationship is purely physical (half-Italian, extremely well-endowed, I'll say no more). Eventually, his lover tires of the hotel business and moves away. Gene's reaction is one of resignation:

*He loves me, he loves me not...* (October 27, 1960)

Back to cruising.

A year later, in an explicit display of loneliness, he conducts a mocking self-interview:

*Gene 1:*

*Why can't I find someone who's interesting, who cares about important things and makes me feel smarter just being around him?*

*Gene 2:*

*Because you're bent and somehow people are picking up on it. They know there's something wrong with you, but they can't figure out what.*

*Gene 1:*

*Sometimes I think I'm going crazy. The world seems stupid and pointless and I can't have the things that matter. Love, a sense of belonging...*

*Gene 2:*

*I repeat. You're <u>bent</u>. You're talking about needing a <u>man</u> but you can't come right out and say it.*

*Gene 1:*

*You know what I mean. You know me better than anybody else.*

*Gene 2:*

*And you disgust me!*

Summer, 1962, a few weeks before my birth (I'm a Gemini), there's suddenly a new boy hanging about 26 Clarence.

*...tall and thin, olive skin, brown eyes. Pompous manner but a sharp dresser. His face is narrow, with a large, hooked nose and whittled cheekbones. Almost wooden expression at times. At other times he seems bored by the whole thing, which I find interesting, considering his delicate position...*

Within a matter of weeks, Gene sounds smitten:

*...seems like every time I think I've got him (Ted) pegged, he does something to thwart my expectations. Today, I spotted him at the end of the bar at Sweeney's and did my eyes deceive me or was he not reading a collection of stories by William Saroyan? Mick and some of the others were at a table so I went over and said 'hello' but eventually I couldn't help myself and wandered up to the bar. Struck up*

*a conversation, mentioned the book and before long, he was telling me about Sinclair Lewis and John Dos Passos!*

*I, on the other hand, foolishly let on I'd never heard those names before in my life and stumbled away in a <u>daze</u>. Asked Terry what he thought of the new guy and he said to steer clear of him, he's a fink for the ginzos in Montreal, here to observe the operation and report back to the Prince of Darkness himself. Making sure we're not stealing more than we're due. I'm not sure what to think. Jack doesn't defer to Ted but he sure takes notice when he's around. Ted definitely seems to have his ear. There's more to this than meets the eye.* (July 14, 1962)

Hoffman cut quite the figure compared to the rest of the outfit. Not merely the way he dressed and his careful, modulated speech ("the voice that bedded a thousand chicks", as Gene puts it). Apparently, he was only half-Irish, which explained his darker complexion. Exotic, mysterious, his appeal stemming from something too subtle to be called charisma, a poise that spoke of great will and strength of character. And it turned out he wasn't lacking in the toughness department:

*...I didn't hear what Mick said but when Ted asked him to repeat it, Mick obliged, clear as a bell: "I said, 'with colour like that, yer mother musta been a wog'." It was either "wog" or "wop" but it doesn't matter because a split second*

*later Mick found himself collapsed against the bar, his arm pulled in tight, protecting his left side, where Ted had just landed a short, vicious hook. Mick's a big man but at that moment he looked like a felled oak. His right arm holding onto the bar was the only thing keeping him upright and despite a fearsome reputation as a pub brawler it was clear he was giving no serious thought to engaging with Ted, who was waiting patiently for him to do just that. The others, including Miles and Gavin, could hardly believe their eyes. Their pal and top bullyboy whipped like a <u>stupid mule</u>. Wouldn't be surprised if he'd busted some ribs. And the whole time this was happening, I was watching Ted and, I swear, his expression never changed, not a flicker. He didn't seem angry or worked up at all…* (September 18, 1962)

From what I knew of Sloane, Ted's one-punch victory was impressive and nervy. Mick, after all, was the Boss's favorite enforcer…

But Ted's actions led to promotion, not censure. Donahue had a soft spot for pugilists and it was high time someone brought Mick down a peg or two.

Gene and Ted were spending more and more time in each other's company and Gene couldn't resist gushing about his new buddy, a man of the world, a man of experience. Bilingual, well-read, cultured. It inspired an impossible fantasy:

*He's a professor at some famous university, his wisdom sought after by scientists, philosophers and heads of state from every part of the world. And I'm his most devoted student and lover, worshipping at his feet and serving as his muse, <u>inspiring</u> and <u>exciting</u> him, body and mind...* (November 2, 1962)

They swapped books, went to movies together and occasionally took drives along the lake or north, into the interior, sometimes as far as Ottawa. Talking, getting to know each other. Gradually Gene began to conceive of the possibility that something was happening between them, something deeper than friendship. Was he reading too much into comments and double *entendres* Ted would occasionally let drop, and were those brushes and moments of incidental contact inadvertent or:

*...is he sending me signals? I'm probably imagining it because I'm so desperate. What else is new? Nothing will come of it and soon I'll be whinging like usual about how no one loves or understands me. I've stopped getting my hopes up and refuse to let my fantasies get the best of me yet again...* (January 12, 1963)

But this time Gene wasn't to be disappointed, this time the gods, in their fickleness, decided to have mercy on him.

February 6, 1963, after a night on the town involving more drinking than usual, the two of them stagger back to Gene's and what begins as a playful grapple on the couch soon turns into something more:

—*gloriously, miraculously, his mouth is on mine and then a flurry of activity as we shed our clothes, roaring with laughter when we see how enflamed* (sic) *we are. No sense of modesty, we fall on each other like a lovesick bride and groom, my living room our wedding chamber. He is agile, dominant, experienced. It's like the dream where I'm his student, kneeling before him, gobbling him up, not caring about anything other than giving him pleasure, making him desire and love me even as he fucks me absolutely senseless…*

The writing gets awfully blue for awhile, the kind of smut that makes you tug your collar and glance around in case there are any kids or sweet, little grandmothers present. The *Reader's Digest* version: after an extended bout of enthusiastic lovemaking involving every available orifice, they collapse to the floor, grab some cushions off the couch and fall asleep in one another's arms.

Then, the inevitable. Waking the following day, looking at each other, first confusion, followed by angry denials and accusations—

Not quite:

*In the morning it's slow, beautiful, rubbing and kissing till we come. Nothing rough, very tender.*

*…Of course, we're aware of the possible consequences but, curiously, we're at peace with it. We shall maintain appearances, play our assigned roles in public. Choose our opportunities whenever we can. Ted clasps my hand in his big, boney fingers. Confesses that he's wanted me from the first time we met and sensing, somehow, that I felt the same. Two kindred spirits. "<u>Anmchara</u>" was the word he used (I made him spell it for me). It's Gaelic for "soul partner" or "soul friend". That's what we are to each other. Now and forever more.*

*He's had many lovers and has much to show me. There's a whole life I've been missing, a concealed world of which I know <u>nothing</u>. I'm eager to learn everything I can, be his best, most brilliant pupil…*

Followed by two pages of romantic twaddle, including an obscene acrostic poem I try my best to purge from memory.

The volume concludes a few weeks later, on a happy note for a change.

Only four more to go, these ones slightly larger than the others; so far, I've avoided the temptation to jump ahead, determined to read them in sequence.

Think of it: they kept their secret for nearly *ten years*. Miraculous in and of itself. You have to admire them for beating the odds.

But they weren't stupid men and were only too aware of how the game was played.

They had to know it wouldn't last forever.

At quarter to eight the phone *chirps* and I'm suddenly overcome with this eerie sense of foreboding, all but certain that it's Eli phoning with the worst possible news.

"Hiya, partner!"

So much for my powers of precognition. "Neil! My God, they let you have a phone?"

"Are you kidding? I get all the amenities here. I'm practically a legend in these parts, kid. Some day they're gonna name a street after me."

"I don't doubt it. But shouldn't you be resting?"

"This is one of those modern day hospitals, me boyo. None of that lying around after surgery stuff. The doctors and insurance companies don't like that. They want us on our feet, mobile, out the door lickedy-split. They don't even take time to use stitches any more, just staple you up and send you on your way. I bet they release me day after tomorrow. Wheel me outside and dump me in the street."

"That's great!"

"You're telling me." Lowering his voice. "Whatever happened to good-looking nurses? There's a couple roaming the halls here who should be wearing hockey masks." I'm laughing like a loon, relieved he seems so sharp and with it, obviously no worse for wear. "Okay, never mind about me. Tell me what I've been missing. And make it quick, Nurse Ratchet will be making the rounds again soon."

I do my best and judging from the number of times he goes "Hmm" I'd say I'm definitely holding his interest.

"I had a pal who rented some gay porn once, just for kicks. He told us afterward it was exactly like, y'know, straight stuff, only the guys were in better shape."

"Interesting observation."

He sounds unreasonably happy for a man recovering from heart surgery. "The more we discover, the better this gets, don't you think? And I don't have to tell ya, these days sleaze sells. And this book's got it, in spades."

"My wife says it's a love story."

"Hmmm…a perverse love story. I like it. She's one smart lady."

"Neil," I plead, "will you promise me you'll ease off for awhile? Will you do that? You've been a great help, a fantastic collaborator, but you have to put your health first."

"Yeah, I read you, but listen, kid—" I hear a woman's voice speaking sharply in the background. "Oh, oh, looks like I'm busted."

"Okay, it's been great talking to you. Remember what I said about—"

"Sure, sure," he says, already in the process of switching off. "Goddamnit, woman, can't you see I'm right in the middle of an important—"

But at that point, we're disconnected.

Poor Neil. That's one battle he isn't likely to win.

I'm glad he seems to be making a speedy recovery. And you know something else? I'm starting to believe he's every bit as indestructible as he pretends. Neil Flory, the *real* Terminator.

Hang in there, old buddy.

## Fifteen

## *Black Hole Sun*

The remaining diaries cover the final decade of Gene's life and from the length and frequency of entries, they were heady times. Browsing through the first of them the following morning, even a cursory glance tells me that his vocabulary and syntax show definite signs of improvement compared to earlier volumes, his observations better elaborated. Was it the influence of Ted? Gene thought so:

*The man has <u>elevated</u> my mind, made me see the world in a totally new light. I am bedazzled, bewitched, totally fucking crazy about him. I feel smarter, <u>stronger</u>, like I'm on some kind of new drug. Addictive and inescapable, the effects* *more powerful than heroin and, in the long run, perhaps even more dangerous and permanent…* (May 5, 1963)

*I never want this to end, go back to the way I was before, <u>lonesome</u> and <u>stupid</u> and <u>pathetic</u>. Thanks to this beautiful, brilliant man (my man!), I am gaining wisdom beyond my years, knowledge that is terrifying and irresistable* (sic), *a light that burns, a secret teaching that immolates me alive…* (August 8, 1963)

"Ted must have been a fascinating person," I tell my wife that night. A long day for her, a couple of home visits with ailing LOLs (little old ladies) and a grueling session at the rehab centre with a new guy, a paraplegic. Car accident, sixteen years old, alcohol related, everyone else in the vehicle killed. That horror show, endlessly replayed in his head, rendering any talk of "healing" superfluous, if not insulting. "He certainly had a powerful hold on Gene. And even though he's an outsider, supposedly a snoop for the Consortium, it isn't long before he's basically running the show. He's got Jack Donahue's ear and tough guys like Dennis Flaherty and Mick Sloane are on their toes around him. Until the Brockville bank robbery, he's the golden boy." We're getting ready for bed, settling down for the night and my wife soon makes it abundantly clear she isn't too keen on all this "Mafia talk" so late in the day.

"They're *not* Mafia," I correct her. "Mafia denotes Italians, specifically Sicily. I read that John Gotti, a big time Don during the Eighties, threatened to decapitate the next person who used the 'M' word in his presence."

"So what do they call themselves?" Pulling back the sheets and climbing in beside me.

"Different things. They're often referred to 'the Outfit' or 'the Family'. Sometimes, a mob guy will introduce someone saying 'he's a friend of ours'. Meaning, hey, don't worry, he's one of us."

"So there's no secret handshake or anything like that?"

"No, that's the Masons. Maybe mobsters click their pinkie rings together or—"

"What I find hilarious is that in the midst of this macho fraternity, you've got Gene and Ted. Gay racketeers. Playing their assigned roles by day, but letting their hair down at night. Right under everybody's noses. Including your father, by the sound of it."

"They had to be amazingly discreet. Never giving anything away in front of the others, keeping their behaviour above reproach."

"I'll bet it caused a lot of stress though."

"Absolutely," I nod. "And then you factor in the added responsibilities once Ted becomes Donahue's main man."

She stops me. "You said everybody had ranks—so what would his be, compared to the two brothers?"

"It's definitely a hierarchy. Lowest of the low are the freelancers, goons on the periphery. Not part of the gang but sometimes employed for muscle and odd jobs. Then there's the soldiers, part of the organization but still at the bottom of the totem pole. After that you have *enforcers*, with a captain in charge of them, and then on up to the street bosses, who run the day-to-day stuff, with usually what they call a 'right-hand man' keeping an eye on the entire operation. From what I'm reading into it, I'd say Ted, before his big fall, was in great shape, almost an untouchable within the Donahue clan. Involved in virtually every aspect of their operation."

"You can't help talking about this stuff can you?" Yawning. Reaching down and cupping my balls. A nimble touch, excellent technique.

I take the hint, turn off the light and focus my attention on matters of a more personal nature.


The next morning, right as I'm about to dive into work, Phyllis phones. No greetings, no small talk. "How are you doing with the diaries?"

"It's a lot of reading but I'm nearly there."

"*Now* are you starting to understand?" The question can be interpreted any number of ways. "I thought maybe if you got to know Gene better, saw things through his eyes..."

"What, I'd stop asking embarrassing questions, come to my senses and forget all about my family's wicked, wicked ways? Is that what you mean?"

"I wish to Christ I knew how I became such a villain in your mind."

"Aw, c'mon, mom, for Pete's sake—"

"Parents do things for the good of their children. Haven't you ever said 'no', denied your boys something and then felt like a complete heel afterward? You're trying to do what's best for them but, in their eyes, it doesn't matter."

A dozen different rejoinders come to mind but I manage to resist them. "I don't understand, mom. Is this a message? A *threat*? What are you getting at?"

"It all comes down to protecting our family. Doing what's necessary to make sure it survives."

The old gal sounds so somber it's making me nervous. "I don't think I see what you're—"

"Finish with those diaries, " she snaps, "and bring them back. Don't forget you're only borrowing them. They belong to *me*."

"Sure, but—" But nothing. She's gone.

I pour myself some coffee, stare out the kitchen window.

Pondering what she said or, rather, what she was trying to tell me.

Gene frequently brags about Ted's growing stature in Donahue's organization, while bemoaning the wasted opportunities:

*He* (Ted) *says if this crew was run as a tight ship, the money would be* <u>*rolling*</u> *in. The bookies aren't being squeezed, ditto the dopers and pimps. Jack's paranoid about calling attention to himself and Ted's sick of it. The outfits in Boston and Philly have everything wired up tight—there's no reason it couldn't be the same here.*

*What they do is approach a local businessman, tell him somebody is putting up fifty gs to whack him and if he wants it taken care of, the price is seventy-five. Or you send some boys in to start a brawl, wreck a bar or restaurant. Next day, go to the owner and say "If you want our protection, make sure this doesn't happen again..."*

*Ted says, if there's no problem, then* <u>*make*</u> *a problem.*

*But with Jack it's like turning an ocean liner. So set in his ways. Like a prehistoric dinosaur. And everyone knows what happened to them...* (October 19, 1963)

There are many entries that basically amount to "Ted did this" or "Ted said that".

Ted even had the temerity to criticize Terry:

*I know Ted deep down likes Terry but his squareness really turns him off. Terry is happy being married, going home to the wife and kids, barbeques on the weekend, the whole <u>bourgeous</u> (sic), <u>middle class</u> existence. Terry's lack of ambition bothers Ted and his "good old boy" personality grates on him too. He can't believe I come from the same gene (ha!) pool as my brother. He says if we were any less alike, we'd belong to different species...*

But it isn't all sweetness and light. Gene and Ted have differing views when it comes to commitment. Ted is far more promiscuous and, by virtue of his experience, has access to numerous casual lovers. He's also, it's clear, the dominant one, a good deal kinkier than Gene, farther out when it comes to his sexuality.

(Ted) *told me once you've done it a hundred times, sex becomes repetitive, "mechanical". From then on it's a case of working harder and harder to find something new to add spice to the mix. <u>Anything</u> to make it exciting again. And it's certainly true that he's more adventurous and worldly than yours' truly. He keeps promising to take me places, meet people willing to do things and have things done to them, but I admit I'm not sure what I think about that. I wonder*

*why we can't try these things ourselves. But he would tell me
I'm just being a "square"...* (November 12, 1963)

Winter, 1963, Ted is dispatched to Montreal on
some nebulous mission for Donahue and Gene tags along.
Once they've dispensed with their duties, they're free to
enjoy the nightlife, visit establishments catering to a wide
variety of tastes and predilections. One place, smack dab
in the middle of the city (albeit reached by a rear entrance,
unmarked in any way) was called *The Catacombs* and, as
Gene quickly finds out, the name is well-chosen:

*...at first glance, just like any other bar until you
noticed the "women" drifting about the room were drag
queens, painted and decked out to the nines. Hair, high
heels, the complete package. Freddie, the proprieter* (sic)*,
greeted Ted warmly, the two of them clearly old friends.
Leading us past the queens, along a corridor, through a
door, down a flight of stairs to the basement. Sweeping
aside a heavy, dark curtain, stepping into a poorly lit
room, dim, red light coming from niches in the walls. No
brighter than candles.*

*Ted took my hand, leading me into that red glow. I saw
shapes, outlines of bodies and could only sense numerous
others. Writhing on mattresses or bent over couches,
thrusting, gasping, naked, ecstatic. Indescribeable* (sic)
*sounds and a smell, a closed in <u>animal stench</u> that made*

*me think of a lion cage at the zoo. I was amazed to discover how stiff I was, in the midst of all that sucking and fucking.*

*As we moved through the room, I could feel people pulling at me, tugging my legs and arms, throwing me off balance. And then all at once Ted was <u>gone</u>, my hand grasping nothing but empty air.*

*The next thing I knew, I was being enveloped from behind, two sets of strong arms over-powering me. I struggled but I was held, subdued, eased to the ground, stripped of my clothes as effortlessly as if I was a child. I felt terrified, excited, multiple hands squeezing and manipulating me, while dim figures heaved and groaned on the floor on either side of me. The smell of sweat and semen was thick, like acrid smoke. Sometimes the hands were too insistent, the kisses too hard. At various moments, fleeting and horrifying, it felt more like rape. I was scared, animal-like, prey to their desires. Enjoying it and hating it.*

*And all along I kept wondering: How many times has Ted been here before?*

Ah, the green-eyed lady, Jealousy: you just knew she was bound to make an appearance, sooner or later.

There's definitely tension within the relationship, the couple enduring their fair share of lovers' tiffs. Part of it was male hormones and aggression, but Gene was also envious of Ted's higher rank within the organization, the difference in status exacerbating their conflicts. Some of these confrontations turned violent:

*Then he made the mistake of telling me I cried like a woman, so I reared back and <u>punched</u> him. He buckled from the impact but now there was blood in his eyes, an old-fashioned Irish fury had taken hold, and he leaped at me, his fists swinging. I dodged or blocked most, not all of the salvo, a cut opening over my left eye, my head <u>ringing</u>. We were down on the floor, grappling, almost face-to-face, our blood dripping onto the carpet. When he lunged toward me again I was afraid he was trying to <u>bite</u> me and screamed, struggling to escape. Seizing my head between his hands, he kissed me, his face coming away streaked with red. He looked gory and beautiful, a warrior god. Like one of those Spartans he told me about, who took male lovers and fought to the death...* (April 14, 1964)

Gradually, Jack Donahue begins to adopt some of Ted's strategies and, as predicted, the cash flow increases appreciably. Which makes Donahue happy and, more importantly, it makes the people in Montreal happy too. The "Consortium" (or, in Gene's shorthand, "the partners").

There are more trips, to Montreal, Hamilton and Toronto, and spring, 1965, a memorable weekend in New York City. The boys do the town up proud. Stay at the

Ritz-Carlton, take in the view from the top of the Empire State Building, see a couple of Broadway shows, including "Hello, Dolly" (boring) and "Fiddler on the Roof" (too many Jews). They also visit a raunchy gay dive called *The Crowsnest*, maybe because of the ancient stuffed parrot perched over the bar. Their waiter has a cock ring, pierced nipples and shaved head.

And let's not forget the floor show:

*—to the tune of The Chantays' "Pipeline", a youngish-looking guy (he was probably older than he seemed), wearing nothing but a Yankees cap, was led out in a chain and dog collar and slowly violated by a man with, and I'm hardly exaggerating, a tool as long as my forearm and as thick as a child's fist. I thought it was* <u>*fake*</u> *but Ted swore it was real. They were both well-oiled but, for the life of me, I couldn't figure out how the kid wasn't split in half...*

Yikes. So that's gay dinner theater.

Ah, my wife's right. Can't be too judgmental. Those were different times, before the horrors of AIDS. Crazy, irresponsible behavior didn't carry the death penalty. Not yet.

Hey, it's the Sixties, *everybody's* getting liberated. Soon Robert Kennedy, Malcolm X and Martin Luther King will be liberated from their lives.

Whoops, there I go again, always looking at the down side. My wife and kids frequently refer to me as "Mr. Fun-Killer". Eeyore, in the flesh.

Assassinations and world crises hardly make a dent on Gene. There was only a brief entry on JFK's murder and so far I think I've come across exactly three references to Vietnam. He was no liberal, taking the cops' side during race riots and civil rights marches. LBJ was a pinko and Barry Goldwater the best President the Americans never had. As for the growing youth movement, more and more visible and vocal during that time:

*…I hate all the hairy-assed music on the radio these days. Too many jungle bunnies and beatniks. I don't like the Beatles or that Dylan guy. Folk music and people protesting the natural order of things, trying to tell us we're all equal and should love one another as brothers. Bullshit! Let's see them try and get away with that kind of stuff over in Russia. They'd soon find out what a few years in the salt mines will do to their cheerful outlook on life…* (September 20, 1965)

…and, later:

*Ted's right: No one ever gained anything by being weak. The meek don't inherit the earth, they haul stones for pyramids, act as serfs for the overlords. He quotes Neitzche* (sic) *regarding <u>will to power</u>. Without it, we're only herd* *animals, stupid sheep, and he and I have much bigger goals and dreams than that...* (December 13, 1965)

Gene goes weeks without mentioning his older brother and when he does, his observations are frequently less than flattering:

*Dropped in to see Terry and family...kids with colds, runny noses, whiny and irritating. Phyllis coping, but I found Terry hiding out in the garage, tuning up his new baby, a convertible Mustang. Looks just like the commercials. Redder than a polished apple and he's got it purring to <u>perfection</u>. But Terry confided he's been taking heat from Phyllis, the kids getting older and she wants him to lead a more <u>normal</u> life. I reminded him what's putting a roof over his head and paying for those fancy new wheels. He nodded but I could see it was wearing on him. Playing around with souped-up cars his only escape, the poor bugger...* (December 23, 1965)

The mid-Sixties was a relatively sedate period: the Donahue clan appeared to be thriving, but Gene only infrequently alluded to his illegal activities, most of his journaling centering around his relationship with Ted. They liked to sneak away, avoid prying eyes by embarking on epic drives through the countryside, sometimes lasting all night. Holding hands, listening to music, going where the mood took them. Frequently ending up in Gananoque, in Joel Stone Park or somewhere down by the water, places Gene remembered from boyhood.

Sitting in Ted's big Chrysler, safe from scrutiny, they could put their heads together and dream of a better future for themselves:

*...no hiding, no pretending, living as we <u>really</u> are. Surviving by our wits, beholding* (sic) *to no man. Independent businessmen, responsible only to ourselves. That's what we're working toward...* (September 2, 1966)

But they're not the only ones dreaming big. During the course of a piss-up with Terry, my father tells him in no uncertain terms that he wants out of the gang and is willing to explore any option to extricate himself. Gene offers sympathy but little more:

*What I <u>don't</u> tell him is that Ted and I have been thinking along the exact same lines, some big score that would allow us to put Jack Donahue and everybody else far behind us. <u>A ticket out.</u> We have our eyes peeled, scanning every horizon for tempting targets. It may merely be wishful thinking on our part but we'll have to wait and see...* (January 3, 1967)

Before the Brockville job, they ponder knocking over an armored car or hijacking a tractor-trailer load of cigarettes. Ted reminds Gene they can use the outfit's contacts in the trucking industry to find the right cargos, routes, drivers willing to play ball, etc.

But will the payoff be worth it? They dither, bat around various ideas, but there's always some excuse to stand pat. What it comes down to is a failure of nerve. Big moves mean big risks, the possibility of going to jail, maybe even getting killed. It had to be worth it; there wouldn't be any second chances.

A substantial chunk of 1967 and '68 appear to be missing—at least one more volume either gone astray or deliberately destroyed.

I don't think it's a major loss. The entries for this period intermittent, perfunctory and I often find myself skimming:

*...Leafs defeat Rangers (pick up $50 in the bargain). Ted coming down with a cold so we called it an early night and...* (October 27, 1968)

*...feeling the strain this week, cleaned out by a couple of dogs they must've rescued from the pound and just tossed on the track...* (June 16, 1969)

*...during the drive up to Ottawa we talked about politics, Ted saying that the worst thing they ever did was make the vote universal. Only an informed and intelligent elite can be entrusted with choosing our leaders—otherwise we*

*end up with mob rule. Which makes perfect sense to me...*
(August 22, 1969)

Despite Ted's objections, Terry is brought into their little conspiracy. Three men willing to risk everything for a shot at getting *out*. They wait, plot, bitch and bicker among themselves and *finally* in early 1971 their patience is rewarded.

But the tip-off for the Brockville Bank job comes from an unlikely source.

*Phyllis*.

One of her cousins is dating an assistant bank manager who likes to brag when he's in the sack. Brockville, despite being off the beaten track, is the repository for a considerable amount of money. Every so often, the figure is very substantial indeed. If a solid crew could be put together and the timing just right, they could stand to make a fortune. Enough, maybe, to buy their freedom and forge a whole other life...

They do some scouting around. The *Savings & Trust* in Brockville is housed in a building of venerable vintage and the security, to put it kindly, is not exactly world class. It's a sleepy community and once the downtown businesses close their doors (six o'clock sharp), there are few souls about.

*It seems too good to be true. I feel like proceeding cautiously but Ted can't wait to start the ball rolling. He says it's an unbelievable setup, as easy as opening a tin can. A once in a lifetime opportunity. He knows guys that can get the job done, absolute pros. He already has someone in mind...* (February 28, 1971)

Plans are set in motion. Ted lobbies hard for Serge Drouin, lauding his abilities as an expert "box man". Contact is made: he's in.

Jack Donahue provides the final stamp of approval.

The heist is the product of months of meticulous planning. They steal most of the equipment they need, draft and redraft their plans. Nothing left to chance.

The Labour Day weekend arrives and, as promised, the haul is huge, even more than expected.

They bust in, load up the loot, shake hands on a job well done.

And from there, it all goes to hell...

*S i x t e e n*

# *Double Talkin' Jive (Get the Money, Motherfucker)*

I t's early afternoon and there are sheets of notepaper littering the couch and the floor at my feet. I write quickly, tear off the finished page once I get to the bottom, go on to the next. Worry about sorting and collating everything later. Lunch consists of snack crackers, cheddar cheese and five or six slices of pepper salami I find wedged at the back of the fridge. Otherwise it wouldn't have survived my omnivorous sons. Quickly devoured and then back at it.

I'm anxious to finish the journals, eager to get to the end now that I've absorbed so much of Gene's character and, at least on some level, have come to know him quite intimately.

I have to say that for the most part I like and empathize with him, keeping in mind that people usually journal in times of crisis or joy. In that sense, it's undoubtedly a distorted, biased portrait. I also acknowledge that in his day-to-day activities Gene helped shake down the region's criminal population as well as intimidating and extorting money from hard-working, law-abiding people in the business community. Hardly the paragon of virtue.

And his devotion to Ted borders on the pathological. That renders him pathetic in my eyes, a captive of Ted's whims and cruelties. Ted takes full advantage of his position, humiliating and manipulating his partner, gloating as he describes his latest sexual escapade, clearly enjoying watching Gene seethe.

Gene tries to strike back, seek out his own conquests but, he admits, these efforts usually result in failure. So he lies, invents trysts, but Ted, sneering, refuses to believe him.

*Ted, my dream-lover, my demon, my punishment…*

Gene realizes he's a fool but can't help himself.

I'm sure many of us know the feeling.

The penultimate diary concludes with a description of the Brockville heist and though the essential facts gibe with Neil's recollections and contemporary newspaper accounts, it's the small details that catch my eye. Gene writes of his super-heightened senses as they enter the building:

*...the stairwell echoing with our footsteps, we sounded like an army instead of four men, moving with absolute stealth and secrecy...brilliant flicker of the torch as Drouin worked his magic, lighting our anxious faces with an alien glow, a comic effect, it was hard to keep from laughing even during such a tense time...*

And once they're inside the vault:

*Stillness. A kind of underwater silence, thick and heavy, that you could wade through. And the <u>smell</u>, the acrid burn of melted metal, but also a musty, old scent, almost like mould. "C'est l'odeur de l'argent," Drouin whispered. "Gentlemen, what you are smelling is moon-ay..." And something about the way he said it or maybe it was out of sheer relief, all at once we were roaring with laughter, hugging each other, wandering the confines of the vault, not touching anything, just looking, enjoying the scale and magnitude of our triumph.* (September 8, 1971)

Athletes and artists describe "peak" moments, a feeling of exaltation so profound, it verges on religious ecstasy. I'm willing to bet the four gentlemen in question were experiencing something very similar.

Unfortunately, it's all downhill from that point on.

The last volume begins in the aftermath of the robbery.

Serge Drouin's capture, while unexpected, is not, at least initially, catastrophic. It still leaves them with nearly two million in stock certificates, bonds and cash to divvy up between them (Donahue taking a sizeable cut). Drouin is a standup guy, no chance he'll rat out his confederates; his Montreal friends will see to his security while he's inside. There are no loose ends to tie up, little risk of exposure.

*...the days pass and Ted and I heave a sigh of relief. We walk down the street and people have no idea what we've gotten away with. It's hard to wipe the grin off my face and even the ominous rumblings we hear from 26 don't spoil the mood...*

The calm doesn't last long.

*...Sloane put the arm on me in Sweeney's, told me that Jack's ready for a face-to-face. Rideau Park. Didn't like the look on Mick's ugly mug and nervously relayed the news to Ted and Terry...*

*...drove out there and I doubt if we said a dozen words between us. It was a good place for a meet, no one likely to be snooping. On the other hand, it was also the perfect spot for an execution (or three) and that didn't sit well. We debated bringing along a piece but knew we'd be searched. If this was just business and we showed up loaded for bear, it*

*wouldn't go over well. We were already in enough hot water, the air around 26 blue. As far as Jack's concerned, we're <u>eight million</u> short, which makes us shit under his shoe.*

*Jack was there, sitting at a picnic table, the others milling about nearby: Flaherty, Sloane, Gavin Hewitt and Tommy Tremaine.*

*"Fucking Murderers Row." Ted looked scared for the first time, which scared me. No sign of anyone we could trust to speak on our behalf. A real kangaroo court...*
(September 18, 1971)

The moment they emerge from their vehicle they are surrounded, searched, frog-marched over to where Donahue waits. He immediately launches into a savage, vitriolic attack, pushing aside the satchel of cash they've brought him, refusing to even look at it. The language is salty, the sentiments unsparing. *Somehow* they will compensate him for his losses, *somehow* they will make amends for this egregious error, *somehow* they will win back his trust and confidence.

In the meantime, they are banished to Coventry. The impression being they should feel fortunate they aren't being handed shovels and led off into the surrounding woods.

And they had to stand there and take it.

—*fucking Mick, looking like he'd just won the lottery, Tremaine and the others, goons with not one functioning* brain in the lot. <u>*Dennis Flaherty*</u> *the new righthand, that was the hardest blow to bear. A brutal, shortsighted man. Jack will not be well-served by that decision. He's denying himself Ted's great mind, as well as the many gifts Terry and I bring to the table, including long, dedicated service. But we're out and there was no point arguing, it would only make things worse. All we can do is accept our punishment and hope to get back in his good graces. But it will be no easy task thanks to Flaherty, a hateful, deceitful man. He'll be working against our interests, never far from the Boss, whispering lying words in Jack's simple ears...*

Then the tough times. The demotions don't sit well, nor do the constant reminders of their lowly status. They're dispatched for coffee and cigarettes, sent to collect Jack's laundry or parcels from the post office or escort Jack's obnoxious kids to a football game in Ottawa...

One indignity after another, week in and week out.

It takes its toll.

There's more carping and sniping back and forth, the two lovers grown familiar enough to know each other's soft spots, where the barbs will go in deepest. Gene gets the worst of it, he's the most vulnerable. After one brawl, they're sufficiently angry to break off relations for nearly two months. Gene is disconsolate at the separation, his journal entries sparse, apathetic:

*A day of no consequence....Another day of no consequence...*

He tries spending more time with Terry but the two have little in common. However, there is one telling incident from late 1971. Terry and Gene are watching the CFL Eastern final in Terry's basement rec room, both of them rooting for the Tiger Cats. For the past two hours they've been guzzling Guinness beer ("shedding a few tears for old Mother Ireland", as Gene calls it). Suddenly:

*Terry gave me a fishy look. "So what's up with you and Ted?"*

*I got goosebumps because I've dreaded this conversation. "What do you mean?"*

*"You guys. What's the story?"*

*"Are you insinuating something, Terry?"*

*He eyed me blearily. "I'm just trying to understand what's going on."*

*I could feel my face heating up, my blood practically boiling. "I don't know what you mean. We're <u>friends</u> and that's it. There's nothing more to it...no matter what might be going through your filthy mind."*

*My brother stared at me for about ten seconds. "I didn't mean that. I only wanted to know when you two were gonna figure out a way to fix things up with Jack." Shaking his head, he turned his attention back to the game.*

*At that moment, I wanted to crawl into a deep, dark hole and die...* (November 20, 1971)

By the end of the year Gene and Ted are reconciled and soon back to their plots and schemes. But something has changed. Terry is sullen, resentful. He feels his association with the botched robbery has permanently damaged his prospects and views Ted as the instigator and source of their troubles.

*Terry buttonholed me at Sweeney's tonight, stone drunk, telling me how much Ted has hurt us and that we need to put some distance between us and him if we want to get anywhere. I felt like murdering him. He must have sensed my hostility because he moved off, mumbling to himself. Did I really tell him that Ted was twice the man he is? Did I really say that?* (January 8, 1972)

Ted's list of enemies is growing, starting with Dennis Flaherty, Donahue's most trusted crony and hatchet man. The old pub brawler loathes Ted, knows he won't be content until he is once again managing Donahue's affairs. He doesn't like the idea of someone looking over his shoulder, waiting in the wings to supplant him. Denny is not a good man to have as an arch-enemy—God knows how many notches he's got carved on his belt, a killer right out of a dime novel. Years later, a *Maclean's* staff writer named Frank Albers wrote a book about him, titled *No*

*Remorse: The Dennis Flaherty Story* (Conifer Press; 2002). That title sums him up.

And Ted is his chief rival and *bête noire*.

One of them has to go.

But Gene and Ted haven't been idle. Ted's smart enough to know that in a power struggle with Flaherty, he is at a distinct disadvantage. Flaherty has a long history with the Boss, the two of them growing up practically across the street from each other.

*Likely suckled by the same wet nurse, the filthy mick bastards,* Gene scrawls in February, 1972, pressing so hard his pen tears the page. It's clear he feels his fate is closely intertwined with Ted's. And Ted is on a collision course with the second most powerful man in the gang. Somehow they need to find an edge, an angle, and, casting about for alternatives, they keep coming back to the idea of a car dealership out west. They crunch the numbers, polish up their business plan, prepare their proposal.

*We have to appeal to Jack's* <u>*greed*</u>*. He's got cash flow problems, the dealership can help with that. I told Ted our motto should be: "We make dirty money clean". He didn't find it very funny. Not much of a sense of humour these days, too fixated on what's been lost, rather than looking ahead to the future.* (March 2, 1972)

Meanwhile, the atmosphere around 26 grows increasingly toxic.

*Sloane and Tremaine have taken to referring to Ted and me as the "fallen angels". They make little wisecracks, ask where our wings are. Sometimes one of them will flap his arms while the other laughs like a hyena. Today I had to grab Ted when he started after them. They barely made it to the elevator in time, wiggling their fingers "toodle-oo" as the door closed…* (March 15, 1972)

*Denny calls down, tells us to bring the boss man's car around and Ted legs it to the parkade. Then he calls again about fifteen minutes later, telling me Jack's changed his mind, take it out and get it washed and waxed instead. And make sure we Armour All the interior, it got missed the last time. I can hear sounds of amusement in the background and want to <u>castrate</u> the fuckers. Ted is waiting in the car and I have to go outside and tell him. The look on his face is something to see…* (March 28, 1973)

The aforementioned cash flow problems only worsen and there is a growing realization that Dennis Flaherty's managerial and administrative skills leave much to be desired. There are rumours of turmoil on the 7th floor, shouting matches, and Ted, especially, has renewed hopes of reinstatement. But Gene is under no illusions:

*Heading in or out, Jack barely glances in our direction. We're never called upon for anything important or treated seriously, just left to cool our heels. Denny is clearly working his spell on him and as long as he has his Master's ear, we might as well be invisible men. If something is going to happen, <u>we have to make it happen ourselves</u>.* (April 19, 1972)

And they try. Once they've got their pitch for the car dealership air tight, they ask to see Jack but Flaherty freezes them out. Not willing to do them any favours, refusing to pass on their messages. It's worse than trying to get an audience with the Pope.

Finally, Gene makes two fateful decisions. The first is to approach Donahue directly, which leads to the confrontation with Flaherty in *Sweeney's*:

*…never saw it coming, a backhand that clipped the side of my face. The place went eerily quiet. But I knew there was no responding, he was holding all the cards, all the power. And he knew it too. A look of total, complete contempt. Grinning as he walked away. Showing his back to my murderous futility…* (May 4, 1972)

Then, with matters clearly reaching a crisis point, Gene bites the bullet and goes to see his brother. He's in trouble and Terry is family, the only man besides Ted he can trust. Ted isn't happy with the gambit, well aware of Terry's feelings toward him, but Gene won't be dissuaded:

*I used the pretext that he's never taken me for a spin in his new GTO and so off we go. After about a mile, he asked me what I wanted to talk about. Not as dim as he seems, my brother. I told him about how the situation between Ted and Denny has grown so bad something has to give. I made up a little white lie and told him Denny made threats against Ted and planned on making the hit himself.*

*Then I asked or, really, <u>begged</u> for his help. I said we had no chance taking on Denny and his crew without him. By the time I was done he was shaking so bad, he had to pull over and park. I could see he was close to tears, as upset and angry as I've ever seen him. He accused me of being under Ted's spell and said the way we were always together was <u>unnatural</u> and people around us wondered what was going on. He said the wisest thing I could do was cut Ted loose and let him fend for himself.*

*I started screaming and yelling, defending Ted and denying everything. I said Ted and I were aware of the malicious gossip and it sickened us. <u>We</u> knew the truth and it didn't matter what anyone else thought. He wasn't convinced but at least lost his accusing tone. He was genuinely worried about me and that took some of the edge off my fury. He assured me he would always look out for me and I believed*

*him. I looked into his eyes and saw how much he still cared.*
*When push comes to shove, my brother will be there for me.*
(May 7, 1972)

Which turns out to be sooner rather than later.

Within a matter of days, Dennis Flaherty disappears.

At first, there's concern that he's somehow been turned, scooped up in the "Program" (as in Witness Protection Program). Donahue sends out search parties, beats the bushes, grilling everyone at 26 about their last encounter with the missing man. Either he's dead or turned rat; whichever it is, Donahue is wild to find him.

Gene's journal entries make it clear he's as in the dark as everyone else. And he doesn't believe Ted is involved, although there's no indication Gene ever puts the relevant question directly to him.

Would he lie? Deliberately deceive himself? Insist Ted didn't do it even if he had evidence to the contrary?

Ted soon finds himself on the hot seat. Everyone at 26 knows of the enmity that existed between him and Flaherty. Donahue's gaze is fixed on him, yet Ted carries on as before, showing up for work and doing his job, refusing to be cowed by the whispers and side glances. But he knows he's a marked man, the realization weighing heavy on him, driving him to distraction:

*Nothing I said or did seemed to please him. He was restless, anxious, endlessly wondering what's going to happen next. I kept telling him "let's get away, take the heist money and hide out in the boonies where no one knows who we are and we can live like free men". But he thought there might still be a way to fix things with Jack, reestablish some trust. He believes he's got protection, thanks to his friends back in Montreal. But to me, the whole thing smells like a power play and that's how Jack must see it too. If Denny doesn't surface soon, Jack will have to act in order to show he's still in charge and that puts <u>all of us</u> at risk. No one is safe...* (May 27, 1972)

Gene's fears and premonitions turn out to be justified.

The following week, he, my father and Ted are back in Rideau Park, only this time the circumstances are far more dire for everyone involved: Ted accused of treachery, the brothers reluctant spectators to what happens next. Phyllis, in her version of events, refused to offer any details of the killing and for that I guess I'm grateful. What little I know, conflicting stories dating back to childhood, is bad enough.

So...now Ted's gone, terminated with extreme prejudice. And Gene, poor Gene, is alone once again.

But when I turn to the next page, there's only a few scribbled lines:

*Put out the candle.*  (June 6, 1972)

And, on the opposite side, undated: *God's punishment on mortal sinners.*

The remainder of the book is blank.

Within weeks of that final, brief entry, Gene's dead too, the coroner's verdict, "death by misadventure". As accurate a description as any.

Exit Ted.

Exit Gene.

Which left Terry. My father.

The last man standing.

*But your old man managed to survive, never fear. Somehow I always walk away in the end...*

Yes, you walked away, kept going...for awhile at least. Until January, 1977. I found you, remember? There's your face again, turned toward me, puffy and distorted from the pain of a bursting heart.

Sorry, Pop, but the evidence is pretty clear: even in your final moments, you failed to achieve anything close to peace. They tried to reassure me that, despite appearances, your suffering was probably short-lived. I've often wondered if it seemed that way to you.

## Seventeen

# Shine A Light

"Hello, *in there...*" My wife, calling through cupped hands from the other end of the table. Smiling at me when I raise my eyes from a spot about six inches above my supper plate. "Welcome back. You vacated the premises for awhile." She indicates the two empty chairs. "Your sons gave up on you."

I vaguely recall some efforts at forced conversation but have no recollection of either of them rising from their seats and leaving the room. "Was I that out of it?"

"Totally. I kept worrying you weren't properly chewing your food. Just scooping it up and shoveling it in." I look down at my empty plate. "Don't bother trying to remember what we had." Laughing at my perplexed expression. "You don't, do you?"

"Sorry—wait! Was it pork chops?" She playfully applauds my perceptiveness. "Ha! So I'm not that bad."

"Really? See how *you* like cooking for a zombie." Grinning at each other. "Okay, point made. I'm not trying to make you feel bad. I take it today was pretty intense. You finished the diaries, right?" I nod. "*And*? Anything new and earth-shattering? Without, of course, giving away any spoilers…"

"I'm almost a hundred per cent certain Gene's death was suicide. I think the loss of Ted was unbearable—and not only that, to actually *witness* his death. I don't think he ever recovered from that horrible day. How could he? How could anyone?"

"He really loved Ted."

"Definitely—obsessed and possessed by him too. It wasn't a healthy relationship but at least it was something. Better than being by himself again…"

"Let's go into the living room, I'll pour us some wine. Leave this," indicating the dishes and detritus, "we'll deal with it later."

"Sounds good to me."

Once we're comfortably settled, I fill her in, summarizing the last few years of my uncle's life, right up until the moment he stood at the end of the dock in Gananoque, his hopes and dreams gone, extinguished. When I finish, she taps glasses with me. "So there's your grand finale. Romantic and tragic. Like *Romeo & Juliette,* except with guys."

"Yeah, I guess so…"

My wife is sharp, not likely to miss such an equivocal reply. "Is there something else? Something you haven't told me yet?" I raise my glass, toasting her intuition. "What? What did you find out?"

"It's not anything specific, just…" I try putting my finger on it but all I can come up with is: "Something's not right."

"You mean your uncle's suicide or—"

Ticking off the points. "First, you've got the bank robbery and the lethal rivalry between Ted and Flaherty. And then Flaherty disappears, so suspicion naturally falls on Ted, which leads to his death and then Gene's…"

"Am I missing something? Doesn't that sort of tie it all together?"

"Yeah, but maybe *too* neatly. This isn't fiction, it's real life. And real life isn't cut and dried like that." Taking a hit of the cold, tart wine. "I guess what I'm trying to say is, I'm not sure I've got it. I think there's something more, something I'm not seeing. The circle isn't closed. Not yet."

"You knew that might not be possible after all this time."

"Probably not," I acknowledge, "but I know someone who might be able to fill in some of the blanks."

"You have to admit, she's been helpful, in her fashion."

"True. But all along I've had a feeling she's been holding back."

"She gave you the diaries."

"That was a distraction," I propose, "she knew I'd focus on them."

"But you think she knows more than she's letting on?"

"We're talking about Phyllis, remember? I'd say that's a given."


She doesn't seem surprised to see me, though I didn't bother phoning ahead of time. I follow her into the living room, toting a black canvas shopping bag. As she takes her seat, I unload the bag, stacking the diaries on the coffee table in front of her. Her eyes flick down the column, doing a quick count. My mother, trusting as ever.

We're seated across from each other, what I can only describe as an expectant silence hovering in the air between us.

"So you're finished then," she finally says. She waits but I don't respond in the affirmative or negative. I don't respond at all. Not a twitch. My impassivity bothers her. "Our family isn't any different, you know. A lot of things go on behind closed doors you never hear about. Even in what you'd think are the nicest, most ordinary homes. No one's perfect."

"I think there's something else." Deliberately being as blunt as I can. "There's more to the story. On some levels it makes sense but then you look at it again and it's way too pat. I don't buy it." She's very still. Not rushing to deny it, no evasions. "You're the only one left, mom. The only one who can tell me what happened."

Another silence, then: "I suppose you're right. A few others might know parts but…I was the one he confided in. The only one he trusted."

"I know dad was there the day Ted was killed. He saw what happened."

Looking at me directly. "Yes, of course. I told you. Him and Gene."

"And he told you about it."

Her face does something, there's a flicker of apprehension. Like any chess master, she can see the way a game is progressing. The moment the board starts tipping in your opponent's favor. "He told me. It was killing him, he lost weight, couldn't eat, couldn't sleep, couldn't carry it around with him any more. The awfulness of that day and then the guilt after Gene died. I think he nearly had a breakdown. It was close. But we talked about it and talked about it and I tried to make him see that Gene was his own man and Ted—Ted reached too high, too fast. He had to fall."

"Sorry, couldn't carry *what* around?"

"He kept calling it a 'blood bargain', even after I tried to explain, *goddamnit, Terry…*" Tearful, furious. "But that day, that awful, awful day…it destroyed them, all of them. Afterward, once Gene realized what happened, what Terry *had* to do, that was it, don't you see? There was nothing left…"

There was an evil vibe inside the car, everyone silent as stones the entire trip. My father was terrified, his guts roiling, and twice Tommy Tremaine had to pull over so he could lean out and puke. The two brothers shared the back seat of a Ford LTD with Charlie Dugan, one of Flaherty's new breed of thugs. Discovered down at Frawley's Gym, punishing a heavy bag and anyone stupid enough to spar with him. A nose like squashed fruit and nothing behind his eyes. He looked like he was itching to lay hands on them.

They were taken deep into the park, up what appeared to be an old logging road. Steep, hardly more than a track, the big Ford needing all its horses to handle the grade.

"Nails" Coughlin had done his job well. Ted Hoffman's palms were affixed to two tree trunks by iron spikes driven through where the meat was thickest. As they looked on, Mick Sloane swung a short bat, connecting with Ted's left knee, so that he sagged, half-collapsing, his shoulders nearly wrenched from their sockets from the strain. Coughlin lived up to his nickname: the nails held fast.

Gene let out a thin, anguished wail and right away Dugan moved up behind him, pressing a pistol to the back of his neck. Terry didn't require similar motivation and they were shoved and jostled forward until they were only a few yards from the proceedings. Somehow, Ted remained standing, his weight mostly on his right leg, the next obvious target. His face was battered almost past the point of recognition, fearful, disfiguring injuries. Gene was biting his fist, blood trickling from his knuckles, moaning, a high, keening sound.

Jack Donahue had chosen to absent himself from the fun and games but the Consortium sent two proxies, Dominic Colombo and, representing the Angels, Frank

"Mother" Kilrea. Their presence meant whatever happened here had been sanctioned by the highest authority. There would be no appeals, no clemency.

Mick Sloane was only too happy to serve as Jack's stand in, greeting the newcomers, cheerfully informing them they were here to bear witness to an execution and expected to pay close attention to what was about to happen. He turned and spat in Ted's ruin of a face, accusing him of murdering Dennis Francis Flaherty in a willful and cowardly fashion. Ted was barely conscious, his features pulped, misshapen, and yet it seemed like he was trying to formulate a denial—

Mick stepped back and with one savage swing of his bat, broke Ted's right forearm. Now Ted came fully awake and *shrieked*, Gene howling along with him, trying to absorb the smallest part of his lover's anguish. Terry was puking again, or trying to; mostly it was dry heaves. Nothing left inside him. Gene was sobbing, pleading with them, defending Ted, trying to be his advocate.

But Sloane had one more surprise in store for them: Ted was a killer but hadn't acted alone. The brothers had known of his plans and either participated in Flaherty's murder or kept their silence afterward. Which meant after he was finished with their accomplice, they would each take *their* turn. Starting with the oldest...

Now fully apprised of their peril, they were forced to their knees, hands on their heads. So close their elbows were brushing. Mick began haranguing them for their disloyalty, pacing back and forth, that lethal bat bouncing on his shoulder.

Somehow Ted summoned the strength for speech. "*...just me...*"

Mick turned, regarding him. Demanded he repeat the statement, and Ted obliged, barely, the words mushy in his mouth. Mick pretended to be puzzled. Hadn't Ted been denying his crime all along? Was he now admitting to the charges?

Ted moved his head in affirmation.

But Sloane didn't believe him. To drive the point home, he broke Ted's other arm.

Ted lacked the strength to scream. All his scalded throat could produce was a low, animal groan. Mick crossed to the brothers, bent down and repeated his pledge to do the same for them when the time came...unless they could convince him they were truly ignorant of Ted's foul designs.

He lifted the bat from his shoulder, admired its grooves and dents for a moment or two, then dropped it in front of them.

"Prove it," he challenged them. "Jack said to give you a chance. Well, boys, this is it. Your one and only chance. Don't take too long to decide. I might change me mind…"

My father was first to reach for the club.

"Sweet Jesus Christ," Gene said. "Ah, Terry, *no*…"

"Leave the head," Mick Sloane advised my dad, "I'm saving that for meself."

I shudder. "He actually said that?"

"Yes. He said it."

"And they did it, didn't they? They had no choice if they wanted to get out of there alive. First dad and then…God, how did Gene…how could he bring himself to…to…?"

She's squeezing her hands together, I can hear the rasp of skin. "Terry wouldn't tell me any more. You'll have to use…poetic license."

"So they—they do what they have to, but soon Gene's dead, which only left dad and—and he…" And at that moment something goes *click*. I look over and she's nodding, confirming it. "Holy shit, mom. He was the only one who benefited, the only one who walked away. He ends up out here, his own dealership, his name in big letters. They let him go. Why? *Why*, mom?" She glares at me, daring me to answer my own question. "It was a *reward*, wasn't it? For ratting Ted out. That little drama in the park, it was *staged*, just to reassure Donahue things were on the up and up. Ted obligingly confesses, they confirm their loyalty and dad gets his fucking dealership. Holy *shit…*"

"You and your sister always thought Terry was weak," she says, "thought I was the one wearing the pants and he was just some good time Charlie. You only knew him as spoiled, snot-nosed kids, getting all the perks, without any of the worries. Big house, swimming pool, spending money. He sacrificed everything for us. That's the way he was. Anything for family. *Anything*."

Call me blind or willfully stupid, but the other shoe finally drops. "My God…*he* killed Dennis Flaherty, not Ted. Ted was completely innocent. Dad framed him and then…let him die like that. To cover *his* crime."

"That's not the way Terry looked at it. He saw Ted as a serpent, poisoning and perverting his brother, leading him astray. For the longest time he tried to deny Gene was queer but inside he knew. It made him sick what they got up to but any time he tried to question their relationship or give Gene advice, Gene would get mad and not speak to him for weeks." I'm listening, but it's like part of me is standing a short distance away, shaking my head in futile denial, refusing to believe what I'm hearing. "The situation with Denny Flaherty reached a dangerous point.

Gene went to Terry and told him, flat out, he and Ted were planning to kill Denny. Terry couldn't believe it, it was *crazy*. He knew Jack would go berserk and there would be a bloodbath. All of us would suffer. So…he acted." She speaks slowly, hardly any inflection, a chill monotone. "It started with him approaching Denny, trying to make peace. But there was drinking, like there always was, and Denny got belligerent, said some things about Gene and Ted…nothing that wasn't the truth but it didn't matter. Terry lost it and shot him, shot him in the head. Drove him out and buried him on the family farm in Lansdowne. Near his old tree fort. Came back and acted like nothing happened. When the time was right, he went to Jack and told him Ted got into his cups one night and confessed everything. He thought by doing that, it would put him and Gene in the clear and save the day. But he should've known it wouldn't be that simple. He wasn't counting on them coming to get him. Being forced to take part…"

"That wasn't in the plan?"

She shakes her head. "That was Jack, like you said, verifying their loyalty once and for all. Poor, naive Terry never saw it coming…" Settling back in her chair. "So. There's your ending. Your father was a murderer and now you can tell the world. Write your book, spill the whole, ugly story, maybe make a few bucks while you're at it.

*Blood money*. Something to soothe your conscience. If you have one…"

That's my cue. There are many things I could say at that moment but the words are jumbled together in my head, an incomprehensible alphabet soup. I'm speechless, unable to formulate a single coherent sentence. I suppose it's shock. But even as I struggle with these latest revelations, there's a realization that Phyllis has been at least three moves ahead of me, as usual. Guiding me, leading me, using misdirection and subterfuge until she maneuvered me into my present, hopeless position. A chess master indeed, toying with her adversary, even as she casually sweeps his pieces from the board.

*Checkmate.*

The drive out to Woodlawn Cemetery doesn't stick in memory. I stop when I'm supposed to, advancing when the lights turn green. It's been ages since I've made this pilgrimage so it takes me a lamentably long time to find the gravesite. A modest rectangle of polished, obsidian-black stone. Accommodation made for Phyllis's mortal remains beside him (Connie and I left to fend for ourselves).

I crouch down, touch the headstone.

Terence Dermot B—

*December 17, 1929- January 26, 1977.*

*Beloved by all who knew him.*

Not a long or distinguished life and he had no great achievements to his credit, nor did he leave much of a legacy. I remember him as a good father, devoted and caring (in his way). His job was bringing home the bacon, not riding herd on the kids or, God forbid, changing their dirty nappies. But, that said, he was an excellent provider and we certainly benefited from his earnings, legal or otherwise.

By some standards, he played the role of Judas, but I would also argue that when the chips were down he stayed true to his family, doing what was necessary, as a father and older brother, to protect them, even willing to *kill* if it meant preserving them from harm.

It's up to a higher authority to judge his various crimes and sins. As for me, I'm resigned to never really knowing the man but satisfied, in my own mind, that whatever he did, he did out of love.

# *C o d a*

## *Music for Airports*

I keep Neil involved as much as possible, e-mailing or texting him semi-regularly, calling to seek clarification on something, updating him on my progress. Or lack thereof.

"Don't worry, man, have a little faith, it'll come," he consoles me from nearly two thousand miles away.

Yes, but *when?*

There's no getting around it, I'm stuck. Not a writer's block, exactly, more like sober second thoughts. Weighing the evidence and trying to come up with some method or approach to this story that doesn't exonerate my father, but at the same time explains his reasoning and ulterior motives. Am I a good enough writer to achieve that fine balance? I have my doubts and, thus, the current stalemate.

Then one Monday in early October I get a call from Neil and from his voice know right away something's amiss. "Do you trust me?" are the first words out of his mouth.

"Absolutely," I affirm, and it's the truth.

"Then listen up..." He sounds almost giddy. "Somebody wants to meet you."

"O-kay..."

"It's all right," he adds hastily, "they're absolutely legit. And I think it's important for you to get together with them. The whole book might depend on it."

"They've got information?" I know I sound suspicious but this strikes me as very odd. And yet at the same time it's *Neil* who's acting as intermediary, so I have nothing to fear, right?

"Big time. And it definitely relates to everything we've been talking about. One other thing: as a further guarantee, it'll be a public place. None of that dark street corner or midnight rendezvous stuff." Pausing. "I can tell from your voice you're hesitant. You really have to trust me on this one, kid, that's what it comes down to. Believe me, you will *not* regret talking to these people."

"All right, Lefty," doing an execrable imitation of George Raft, "where do they wanna make the meet?"

He laughs. "Atta boy. At the airport."

"Here? Saskatoon airport?"

"You got it. Show up three o'clock tomorrow afternoon, go to the main terminal, find the *Tim Horton's*—"

"I know the place."

"—take a seat and wait."

"How will they know me?"

"That's their problem. I just told you all I know. Everything they told me. The rest is up to you."

"Okay, I guess that'll have to do. I'll be there, three o'clock sharp. You've got me really, really curious, Neil." Then, because I haven't asked for awhile: "Hey, how are you feeling by the way? Getting around more?"

"I do okay. I just have to accept the fact I'm old and everything takes ten times longer to accomplish. Once I make that adjustment, I'll be fine."

"Well, you hang in there."

"Will do. Take care, kid. And let me know how it goes tomorrow."

I switch off, lean back in my office chair, prop my left foot up on the desk. Standard reflective pose.

What am I to make of this? A red herring, a clever ruse…or *maybe* just what I need to kick-start this family memoir or whatever the hell you want to call it. Once I came face to face with my father's murderous duplicity, I admit it, I backed off, a grievous display of artistic cowardice on my part. I haven't been able to bring myself to tell Neil who it was that set events in motion and then stood by and watched an innocent man die a horrible death. And if I can't tell *him*...

I have to hand it to my mother, she played her hand beautifully. Giving me the diaries, allowing me to piece everything together myself, unlock the mystery, discover the awful, inescapable truth that the man who helped conceive and raise me had committed the ultimate sin. Just telling me wouldn't have been enough, I had to find out through my own cleverness and intuition. That was essential to the scheme.

Now I'm cursed with the knowledge that if I *do* write my book, my father's name will be forever tarnished, our family's privacy violated, decades old crimes revisited and pored over for as long as the public's interest holds.

And for what? Money? A crack at the non-fiction bestseller list? Maybe a movie option (hey, at least made-for-TV)? The big time...

Ah, Phyllis, you clever gal. You carried the burden for so long.

Now you've decided it's my turn.

It's a few minutes past three. The food court adjacent the *Tim Horton's* kiosk is half full, people either awaiting their departures or the arrival of loved ones on an incoming flight. I've been sneaking glances but never catch anyone staring back at me and in my present mindset *everybody* appears suspicious.

I've chosen a spot roughly in the middle, halfway to the windows overlooking the runways. As I wait, I experience that cavernous, ambient soundscape peculiar to airport terminals: an oceanic murmur of voices, shuffle and drag of passing feet, the occasional (usually unintelligible) announcement that always makes everyone sit up, straining to decipher the gibberish.

At seven minutes after three I see him striding toward me, flanked by a harried aide. The pair present a striking contrast—short, round and sweaty *versus* tall, suave and immaculate—but I hardly have time to think about it before they're at my table and the latter is offering his hand.

"I know you," I say. Because I do.

Never mind his name or party affiliation, the gentleman in question is a rising star on the political scene, a real up and comer. Started out in the Ontario legislature, nabbing a plum cabinet post, making the right kind of waves, earning favourable attention. Then on to Ottawa, several terms in Parliament under his belt already;

articulate in both official languages, his high profile creating speculation among pols and pundits, many of whom predict a future run at the party leadership.

One day, the guy shaking my hand could be prime minister.

But…why is he here?

I watch in amazement as he pulls out a chair and sits down, radiating charm and self-confidence. "I'm glad," he replies, "saves time on introductions." His perspiring assistant stations himself at a nearby table, close enough to leap on my back and yell for help should I prove to be a threat. Not exactly my idea of a bodyguard. I must look pretty bewildered because Mr. X chuckles. "I'm guessing you weren't expecting this."

"Not by a long shot." Ruefully: "I'm gonna kill Neil for not telling me."

"He was sworn to secrecy," raising a finger to his lips. "Ruining the surprise was explicitly *verboten*." Glancing at his watch, a Tag Heuer. Flashy, expensive. Nothing but the best for the man with the Right Profile. "Sorry, but we've only limited time and a lot of ground to cover."

"If you're trolling for votes…" I joke lamely.

No smile this time. "We need to talk about this project of yours."

"My...project?" He nods. "Well, first of all I'd better explain, at this point it's barely even—"

"There's an old Irish saying, do you know it? It goes: *he who loses money, loses much; he who loses a friend, loses more.*" His direct eye contact is unsettling; I'm starting to sweat as much as his assistant. "I'd like us to be friends but I'm worried this book of yours could complicate matters. It seems there are parts of it that broach on certain individuals and incidents that might cause me...embarrassment. Unwanted attention."

I'm genuinely mystified. "I can't imagine how. It's basically a—a family history. My father, his brother—"

"Yes, but they had friends, didn't they? Associates. Men who gained notoriety for behaviour that was not always...exemplary."

"Absolutely," I agree. "But, see, that's only part of the story—"

"But the part with special significance to *me*, I'm afraid." Consulting his fancy timepiece again, a man much in demand.

I'm flummoxed. "*You?*"

"A maternal uncle. My mother's brother. Someone I vaguely remember from childhood. There are pictures of him bouncing me on his knee. As I said, quite embarrassing."

*Oh, shit.* "Ah. That wouldn't be Uncle Jack, would it?"

"Indeed. Uncle Jack." We regard each other.

"Family secrets…they can be a real bitch sometimes, can't they?"

He throws back his head, brays with laughter. "That's right. You're exactly right." Performing a brief drum roll on the tabletop with his index fingers. "Which brings us to the crux of the matter."

"My book that isn't a book."

"Not yet, anyway." Eyeing me but leaving the rest unsaid.

"So you want to me to ditch it, find another project or…what? You'll use your influence and see it never gets published?" He brushes off that suggestion but then something else occurs to me. "Or maybe you're *really* serious. Some of your uncle's friends still mobile, a little long in the tooth, maybe, but—"

He raises a hand. "Please. You're being silly and not only that, insulting my intelligence." There's an edgier aspect to him now and I'm alert to the change in his demeanor. "Go ahead, write your fucking book, you think I'm trying to stop you? But here's the thing, our little compromise." Unconsciously, I'm leaning in closer. "It's a work of fiction, get it? Like those Indian stories of yours.

Something you made up. No more true to life than, say, *The Godfather*. Or *Jaws*."

It's like the rest of the world has faded out and it's only the two of us, alone in our cone of silence. "Am I getting this straight? It's okay to write my book, I just can't call it a true story?" He nods and I try to process this new angle. "But that means totally rethinking the entire—"

He makes a small, almost subliminal motion and *instantly* his roly-poly assistant materializes beside us, placing a slim file folder before him, receding just as quickly. "But it solves our problem, don't you see?" Resting a hand on the dossier but leaving it unopened, at least for now. We both know what's in there is a game changer. Whatever that skinny file contains scares the mortal piss out of me. "You would agree that certain things should be kept under wraps, even in a free society. State secrets. Plans for advanced weapons, technical innovations, information that would do genuine harm if, say, the wrong people got hold of it." I'm nodding, unable to take my eyes off the folder. "You and I have bright futures ahead of us. There's no reason why anything should hold us back from our rightful destinies. The past is the past. Let's leave it that way."

Then he opens the file.

None of us lead blameless lives. Like Freddie Mercury says: *And bad mistakes/I made a few…*

It's the same for me, for you. For all of us.

It doesn't matter what's in the file. It could be anything. Evidence of a dalliance I once had with an attractive student, perhaps even pictures of a love-child, looking a lot like Connie at the same age.

Or an unreported hit-and-run, too drunk or too scared to stop and find out what I'd done.

Then there's the fact that the family home, the dealership, my mother's investments and retirement savings, could all be considered the proceeds of crime. What would Revenue Canada say about *that*? Our financial affairs definitely wouldn't stand up to close scrutiny—poor Phyllis might be out on her ear.

He could easily gain my cooperation if not outright compliance by finding something on Connie or, as unlikely as it seems, my wife.

One of my boys a small time drug dealer.

Pick whichever you like. Or substitute one of your own.

We all have secrets to keep.

Some we prefer taking with us to the grave.

I walk into the alcove, stand behind my chair. Swing it around and settle into it, wheel it in closer to my workstation. A black binder hinged open beside the keyboard, containing God knows how many pages of notes. A file box wedged under the desk, full of clippings and magazine articles, some of the books I've sought out for my research stacked off to the side.

What will my wife think of this sudden change in direction, a memoir all at once transformed into a crime novel? Will she understand? And how about Neil?

I'll tell them I've made an aesthetic decision, that a meticulously researched, factual account no longer interests me. Instead, I intend to write a book that blurs the distinctions between truth and fiction, one that sets out right from the beginning to deceive. Change the names, locations, muddy the water, obscure or ignore actual events.

My father had his sayings too and one of my favorites is: *Every man's a liar, at least the ones that still draw breath.*

Seems fitting he should have the final word.

After all, he helped make me who I am, a professional liar, the latest in a long line.

# *A f t e r w o r d*

## *by Cliff Burns*

I might as well come clean: it was never my intention to write a straightforward family memoir.

Right from the beginning I knew that *Disloyal Son* would not be confined to actual events. If the story showed signs of stalling, becoming too dull and static, I gave myself the authorial freedom to embroider, exaggerate or just *make shit up*.

You want the truth? The truth is my father frequently fibbed about his past, including his war record (nonexistent), to make up for a life of no significance, which he basically pissed away. *Two* of his brothers died under strange circumstances, so strange that no one seemed to know exactly what those circumstances were. The stories kept changing...which made their deaths even *more* mysterious to my sisters and I.

Secrets and lies...every family has them. The things we conceal, the deliberate falsehoods we tell to cover our tracks.

Oddly enough, digging into the past, attempting to find out what really happened to my uncles, has never particularly interested me. I've lost touch with that side of the family and doubt very much if I'll ever get the goods. My Aunt Virginia, dad's last surviving sister, died a few years ago—we kept in intermittent contact and though I brought up the subject of her brothers on at least a couple of occasions, she never responded, or even acknowledged my queries. As tight-lipped as Gloria, her counterpart in the book.

Well, who's to say the "mystery", if it ever *is* solved, would amount to much? The truth may be surprisingly prosaic, even mundane. Maybe it's better not to know.

I'll wager my version is far more satisfying, in every respect.

I'm a literary man, after all, not a historian. What Werner Herzog calls "the accountant's version of the truth" holds no interest to me. Frankly, I'm of one mind with the reporter in "The Man Who Shot Liberty Valence": *when the legend becomes fact, print the legend.*

And when the facts get in the way of a good story, well…

Facts.

Truth.

We'd better be careful here because we're on mighty shaky philosophical ground.

I'm not convinced there's any such thing as a "true" story. Apropos to that, I also believe that memory is the ultimate unreliable narrator. No memoir or autobiography, regardless of how well-meaning and ruthlessly candid it purports to be, is completely objective, factual and photographically accurate.

I remind you that these books were written by human beings with biases, personal axes to grind…and personal foibles to gloss over. And if there's any kind of emotional or physical trauma involved (and there invariably is), forget it. Horrific, soul-damaging events are like black holes: they distort everything around them. Space, time, even reality itself bent and warped, fundamental laws of science disregarded, rendered moot.

And let's be honest: *we all lie*. We can't help it. We lie because it improves the anecdote, adds punch to the punch line or so that we appear more noble/courageous/ witty than we actually are. We lie to cover acts of wrongdoing and sins of omission. For some of us, lying is a form of self-protection. For others, it's a way of life.

Sometimes we make up lies and call them *memories*. Convincing falsehoods that eventually become part of our personal myth.

So if an account isn't, by the strictest definition of the term, "true", what do you call it? What's the line between fiction and non-fiction, between real, verifiable incidents and a conscious (or unconscious) manipulation of details and context; at what point do we sacrifice veracity for verisimilitude?

My contention is that there *is* no line, that a scrupulous adherence to "just the facts" is impossible. Even the most intimate journals conceal as much as they illuminate. The selection of what to include and what to omit is, in and of itself, a *creative* exercise. Providing a cohesive narrative, believable characters, realistic dialogue, any kind of structure or timeline…these are the same aesthetic dilemmas that confront every writer, regardless of their chosen genre.

\* \* \* \* \*

In the final analysis, dear Reader, all I owe you is a good story, a well-told tale. A yarn, a corker, one to share around the campfire or enliven a family trip. Entertaining and thoughtful, inhabiting a universe that is consistent, complex and authentic.

A good story, yes: meaning one with a beginning, middle and something resembling a conclusion. With a plot that transports you, takes you on a trip to the far reaches of credulity (while cautioning you not to look down and spoil the effect).

And if it's *my* yarn, I'll tell it any damn way I please. By the time I'm finished, who knows where the lies begin or end? I stopped making strict distinctions like that a long time ago. My life history so scrambled up with my writing I'm no longer certain what really happened and how much I've imagined, experienced or…adapted.

Because in all honesty I've been making shit up for as long as I can remember. I invented my entire childhood, spending much of my time in a hermetically sealed bubble of reality built out of books and vivid daydreams. And I told many, *many* lies, to compensate for a cowardice exacerbated by fears and insecurities brought on by an inescapable sense of powerlessness. I felt gripped and mauled by forces beyond my comprehension and lived in constant fear of catastrophe and doom. I devised scenarios to distract and amuse myself but also, I think, to attain some kind of *control* over my creations. Assembling a motley cast of characters, concocting nefarious storylines to challenge and confound them…all too aware that I possessed the ultimate power over my charges, the capacity to mete out life…or death.

Some of these episodes I wrote down and *that* was mind-blowing—like "Moon-watcher" touching the monolith at the beginning of "2001: A Space Odyssey". I've always been an avid reader and so putting my thoughts on paper, assembling universes that conformed to my own peculiar specifications…well, talk about intoxicating. And I've never gotten over it.

Most children grow up and lose their world-building aspirations. As the years went by, mine became grander and *more* detailed. By refusing the laurels of adulthood I've managed to retain an active, mischievous imagination. In many ways I'm an eternal twelve-year-old, forever on the cusp of adult cares and responsibilities but always managing to dodge most of them with a nimble aptitude Tom Sawyer would admire.

How much of this or *any* book is true?

I respond by insisting the question is puerile, irrelevant. You might then accuse me of evasion but I would counter that my motives are, for the most part, honorable and that it is my firmly held view creative endeavors should seek to *illuminate*, not disguise or obscure…and that inner truths and insights always trump dull recitations of fact.

Besides, don't the annals of history prove human beings love an accomplished liar? Think of the con men and charlatans and snake oil salesmen we've followed like lemmings, even if it meant our doom. If nothing else, these individuals keep us enthralled with their antics, removed from everyday concerns, the unpleasant truths that are too tangible and distressing to ignore…or forget.

C.B.
*(February, 2015)*

## About the Author

Cliff Burns is the author of a number of previous novels and short story collections, including *So Dark the Night*, *The Last Hunt* and *Sex & Other Acts of the Imagination*. His work has been featured in magazines and anthologies around the world and adapted for radio and stage. He lives in western Canada with his wife, artist and educator Sherron Burns.